MURDER AT THE CROQUET CLUB

A ROSE BLAIR MURDER MYSTERY

JUDY KEIGHTLEY

ISBN-13: (Paperback) –978-0-9919187-1-3
Publisher: Judith Keightley

In memory of Judith Gooding
A good friend and mentor.

PROLOGUE
BAYFIELD

In silent horror Rose looked at the body of her dear friend slumped over a grey headstone. Her eyes were wide open and her face, even in death, registered a look of sheer terror. A metal arrow had pierced her chest with such force that the tip had literally impaled Mary to the gravestone set in the ground behind her...

ONE

T om, Tom, wake up," Rose said as she elbowed her husband gently in his ribs. "It's seven thirty and isn't Doug picking you up at eight?"

Tom grunted and rolled over. As Rose got out of bed and pulled open the blinds the bright sun bathed their bedroom in lightness so much so that Tom buried his face under the duvet to stop the sun from blinding him.

It was a beautiful August morning and the garden looked particularly charming in the early sun. Rose walked out of their bedroom and padded down the hallway to their kitchen where she filled the kettle with water and prepared to make a pot of tea. It was blissfully quiet and for once the house was empty apart from Tom, herself, and, of course, Ben their faithful black Labrador. Thinking of Ben, Rose wondered where their beloved dog had gone. *Normally he wanted to go outside first thing in the morning, so where was he?*

It was then that Rose noticed that the back door was open, and just as she was registering this Ben came charging in jumping up to give her a big, wet lick. He then ran off to the bedroom to jump on the bed.

That will wake Tom up, Rose thought as she closed the back door. *But who had let Ben out in the first place?* A chill of fear ran down her spine as memories of the previous summer came flooding back. The scarecrow hanging from the pear tree had looked so real then, Rose would never forget the whole affair, ever.

She poured out two cups of tea and proceeded to carry them into the bedroom where Tom was now lying wide awake with Ben at his side.

"Here you are, love. Don't forget that you have a game of golf with Doug this morning. Oh, by the way, did you let Ben out into the garden?"

Tom sat bolt upright and glanced at the bedside clock saying, "Goodness, it's almost 8 o'clock. Doug will be here any minute now." With that he leapt out of bed and disappeared into the bathroom. Rose could hear the tap water running as Tom quickly brushed his teeth and threw on his clothes.

As if on cue, the doorbell rang. It was Doug, punctual as ever. Rose handed him a cup of tea and told him that Tom would be out shortly.

"Doug, you didn't come by earlier and let Ben out, did you?"

"I could hardly come into your house, Rose, as the front door was locked. Why the serious face?"

"Well...oh, it doesn't matter, I'm sure that there is a perfectly simple explanation. Oh, here is Tom. Have a good game you two. See you this afternoon."

Tom kissed Rose goodbye and the two men left, leaving Rose drinking her morning cup of tea. No sooner had they departed when the telephone rang.

"Oh, hi Mary...Oh my gosh. I completely forgot, yes, I'm still coming, just might be a little late. Just go ahead and practice without me. I'll be along in about 20 minutes."

Rose put the phone down and looked at the clock. *Why is it,* she thought for the umpteenth time, *why is it that we are so dictated to by the clock.* However, it had been her own fault for forgetting that she had planned to meet her friend Mary at the croquet courts at 8:00am. They both had wanted to get a practice in before their game at 8:45. It was now 8:15 and there she still was, in her dressing gown.

Mary had joined the Croquet Club the same time as Tom and her. Whereas Tom had mastered the game quickly, Rose had struggled with getting control of her mallet. In fact, Mary and she were as bad as each other, or as good, which is what Mary always said, "We're as good as each other," and Rose had thought to herself, *yes, we are good for each other.*

Mary had only moved to the village of Bayfield less than a year ago and they had met each other at fitness class. She was a little younger than Rose, small and wiry with eyes that twinkled like diamonds and a smile that would warm the coldest of winter mornings. They had instantly become the best of friends.

Indeed, it was Mary who had helped Rose make the canapés for Paul and Atsuko's wedding.

They had made little cucumber cups filled with an assortment of fillings, fig phyllo pastries, goats cheese tarts, cream cheese stuffed strawberries, fruit kebabs, bacon wrapped chestnuts, tiny blinis with smoked salmon and cream cheese, and the list went on. They had had such fun together, giggling like schoolgirls when several of the guests had asked for the name of the caterer.

That was back in June and now it was August, and Rose only had Jessica and the girls left to visit one more time before the Labour Day weekend and the beginning of another school year.

Putting on her white three-quarter length pants and white short sleeved top, Rose grabbed her sun hat from the lobby cupboard. Although it was early in the morning, by nine the August sun would be beating down on their heads. She grabbed a water bottle and a little bag of orange and cranberry scones that she had baked the night before.

Mary didn't like baking, although, she was an excellent

cook. Rose always baked too many muffins or scones and had got into the habit of bagging up surplus goodies to give to Mary.

Right, everything is ready, Rose thought, *I should get to the Croquet Club in time for a bit of a practice before the game. I must lock the front and back doors before I leave.*

Ever since the burglary the previous year, Rose had tried her hardest to remember to lock up the house before she left.

Her friend, Susan Parker, the Inspector, had really reprimanded her for not locking up the house telling her that predators lurked everywhere.

It was truly a beautiful day. There was not a single cloud in the azure blue sky. The air was clear and crisp, and the birds were singing. Rose drove down Short Hill to Highway 21, then took a left down Jane, drove past the pretty Anglican Church on Keith Crescent, and swung onto Sarnia Street.

She then took a left down David Street following the dirt road around the tight bend until it came out in front of the Croquet Club, one of Bayfield's best kept secrets. Indeed, Tom and Rose had lived in their village for five years before either of them had even known about the existence of the club, let alone the geographical whereabouts.

Rose pulled into the car park and immediately saw Mary's blue Honda Civic parked in the car park. Looking out over the immaculately manicured lawns, Rose could see no sign of her friend.

Shrugging her shoulders, she walked over to the storeroom where spare mallets were kept. She opened the cupboard and selected a suitably sized mallet, then poured herself some water and carried it over to the canopied picnic tables.

Where could Mary be? Rose thought and then she saw a mallet lying on the grassy slope leading up to the cemetery which bordered the one side of the Croquet club.

Maybe she's gone to look at the graves, Rose thought as she wandered over to where the mallet lay nestled in the grass. She picked it up and proceeded to walk up to the fence.

All of a sudden Rose spied a piece of white cotton attached to a protruding barb of the fence. Just as her mind was registering the thought that it looked like a piece of material, she saw a foot protruding from behind a gravestone.

Rose carefully climbed over the fence and walked slowly over to where she had seen the foot. She already knew before looking that the shoe on the foot was a white Croc, identical to the one's that Mary always wore for playing croquet.

In silent horror Rose looked at the body of her dear friend slumped over a grey headstone. Her eyes were wide open and her face, even in death, registered a look of sheer terror. A metal arrow had pierced her chest with such force that the tip had literally impaled Mary to the gravestone set in the ground behind her.

Rose stood there numb. It was as if all time stilled into a single, horrific moment. She had not realized it but inadvertently she had held in her breath, and now she exhaled it in one large whoosh. Rose was galvanized into action. Stumbling back to the fence, stepping over it, and running back to the storeroom where she knew there was a phone, out of breath, and still in a state of shock, Rose dialed 911.

INSPECTOR SUSAN PARKER turned left at the junction between Highway 8 and Brucefield. It had been a quick and easy drive from her Richmond Street Major Crimes Unit Headquarters, only one hour and Bayfield, her destination, was a mere 8 minutes away. As she drove on through Varna, Susan started to have mixed feelings about what lay ahead. Last year had been so stressful.

The murder on Bayfield beach and the subsequent uncovering of the Kincardine, Wingham scam, and not forget her disastrous relationship with Jim Reynolds, all served as a jolting reminder to Susan that all was not always what it seemed in the sleepy village of Bayfield.

Initially when she had received the phone call from the OPP detachment outside of Goderich requesting her assistance, Susan had been delighted at the thought of reacquainting herself with the attractively quaint village.

Last year she had discovered that her old university friend, Rose Blair, now lived in the village and the two of them had spent some time catching up on their lives since leaving university. Rose was married to Tom, who, under different circumstances, Susan would have loved to have gotten to know more intimately.

Indeed, there had been that one kiss which had hinted of deeper things, but Tom had firmly attested to his love for his wife, Rose. Susan felt embarrassed remembering the incident and was determined to keep her distance from Tom.

As she reached the ridge at Goshen Line, Susan could see Lake Huron.

The blue water shimmered under the morning sun. Several small sail boats were out. It would be a perfect day for sailing.

She almost missed the turning to the cemetery but, just in time, Susan made the right turn and drove down the leafy, gravel road until she could see an area that had been cordoned off with yellow tape.

There were two O.P.P. cars parked by the side of the tape, and as Susan got out of her car, she could see the body of a woman lying slumped against a gravestone. Two police officers were standing by talking in hushed voices.

"Good morning. My name is Inspector Parker, and you are?" Susan said as she extended her hand to be shaken.

"Oh, I'm Constable Elliot and this is Constable Brown." Both men extended their hands out to shake Susan's.

They don't look old enough to be policemen, flashed through her mind as she shook their hands and then pulled out a pair of white latex gloves. "So, who discovered the body?"

"Er...ma'am, a Mrs. Rose Blair. She is over there the other side of the fence. It's a croquet club."

Susan walked over to the fence and looked onto what appeared to be a bowling green with tightly mown grass. Hoops were placed in a set format.

At the end of the green was a car park where a blue Honda Civic sat alongside a Volvo. Susan recognized the Volvo as her eyes sought the owner whom she knew, Rose Blair.

She saw her friend sitting with her head in her hands under the sun canopy to the left of the croquet court.

"Constable Elliot, walk over and tell Mrs. Blair that she can go home now. Someone will interview her later on today."

Constable Elliot was thirty with a face that looked like a fresh-faced teenager. His hair was buzz cut and his eyes were a startling blue. He nodded his head and set off across the fence to speak to Mrs. Blair.

"Right. Constable Brown, any idea who we have here?" Susan said while still bending over the slumped body.

"Yes, ma'am. Mrs. Blair identified her as one Mary Stokes. She is, um...was, a friend of hers. They were meeting here to practice croquet. The blue Honda belongs to her."

"Thank you, Constable. Forensics should be on their way. Look, I'm going to leave you here while I go into the village to set up an incident room."

Before Susan set off, she took one more look at the dead woman. She was slumped over a gravestone with what looked like a long, metal arrow pierced through her chest. Her face was contorted into a mask of terror. Her legs were bent at an unnatural angle. It looked as if the force of the arrow had literally blown her backwards and impaled her to the stone gravestone.

By the looks of things this had all the signs of a planned execution.

. . .

ROSE DROVE HOME IN A DAZE. Everything felt unreal. Could her friend Mary truly have been murdered at the Croquet Club or was it all just some nasty nightmare and she would awaken from her dream and all would be normal again?

She turned down Charles Street and drove to Bayfield Terrace. As she approached her home with its white picket fence and honey-suckle cascading over the porch, her heart lifted and some of the fog of the morning cleared.

Ben was waiting for her at the door, his tail wagging and big head nudging her for attention. Rose walked into the kitchen and made herself a cup of tea.

She looked at the clock. It was eleven o'clock. She had been at the Croquet Club for two hours. Tom wouldn't be home until at least one, yet Rose longed to be held in his embrace and to cry on his shoulder.

The shock of finding Mary dead had really impacted Rose's psyche. She just could not wash away the image of Mary's terror etched face, mask like in death.

Rose decided that she would just have to bake away her shock. She started off by making a batch of her cranberry and orange scones and then, for a special treat, she made Ben a tray of liver dog biscuits.

The last baking tray of bone shaped cookies was just coming out of the oven when there was a knock on the door. Ben ambled over and barked just as Rose opened the door.

Susan Parker looked tanned and beautiful wearing a pink, silk blouse tucked into a navy-blue pencil skirt and a matching jacket. Her short, blonde hair from the previous year had grown to a jaw length bob cut which Rose thought was softer and more feminine than the Annie Lennox look that she had sported before.

"Rose, it's been too long. How are you?" Susan hugged Rose warmly and followed her into the kitchen.

"What a delicious smell. I see that you've been baking."

Rose smiled and nodded. "Would you like a cup of coffee and a scone?"

"How could I resist? Yes, I'd love a coffee, but this unfortunately is not a social visit. I'm sure that you know what I've come about?"

Rose felt her eyes well up with tears. For a while she had managed to forget about the horror of the morning, but now she was being faced with the whole ordeal all over again. She took a deep breath and answered softly.

"Yes, Susan, you have to ask me questions about my friend Mary, but we can do that over a cup of coffee? Here, let's move into the sunroom and I'll bring out the hot buttered scones and coffee."

Rose led Susan into the cozy sunroom. She loved this room. It was the most used area of the house. Susan sat down on one of the soft love seats and Ben immediately jumped up and nestled up beside her resting his big head on her lap.

"Oh Ben, get off you naughty boy." Rose cried.

"I really don't mind, Rose, he's welcome to share the sofa with me. But come on and sit down. I do need to ask you some questions."

Rose placed the tray with a coffee pot, milk jug, two pottery mugs and a plate of buttered Cranberry and orange scones onto the coffee table and then sat down on her favourite cane chair.

"Ok, Susan, fire away."

"Well, we know that the deceased was your friend Mary Stokes and we also know that you were the one that found her. Is there anything else that you can tell us about her? For instance, had she been acting differently or been nervous lately? Had there been any significant change in her behaviour?"

Rose sat still and contemplated her hands and then spoke again with a very small voice.

"I had only known Mary for one year and in that time I felt that I still didn't really know her. She was a very private person. Don't get me wrong, she was lovely, warm, and the most kindhearted woman you're ever likely to meet, but she rarely divulged anything about her past. All I know is that before moving to Bayfield she had lived in Guelph. She was married before, but I know nothing about her previous life."

"We found in her car a purse which carried her driver's license. We'll be able to track quite a lot down through that but I'm going to set up the incident room first and then I'll send Constable Elliot around to check her house. Did she have any pets?"

Rose let out a small cry. "Oh yes, poor Puff. That's her dog. She loved Puff so much. I'll go around and bring Puff back here. Please don't let him be taken away to the Humane Society. In fact, could you call me when the Constable goes to Mary's house and I'll pop over then and collect Puff?"

"Okay Rose, if you're sure that you don't mind keeping the dog. It doesn't sound as if she had any near or close family around here, but if we find a relative who would like to have the dog then I'm afraid that you will have to relinquish him."

"Of course, I totally understand." Rose said as she handed her over another cup of coffee. Susan departed after demolishing three of the scones and drinking two cups of coffee.

As Rose cleared away the tray and washed up the plates and mugs, she once again had a flashback to her friends' dead body and contorted face. Tears began to roll down her face and a deep sob was wrenched from her throat. Ben, on hearing this, padded over and nudged Rose with his wet nose.

"Oh Benny Boy, I already miss Mary. What happened to my dear friend?"

By the time that Tom arrived home Rose had composed herself, in fact, she got busy again by cooking for the weekend.

Abby and Ella, their darling grandchildren, were coming to stay while Jessica and Rob had a weekend together in Toronto.

She always made 'Grandma's special spaghetti pie' and a dark chocolate and walnut cake when they visited. When Tom entered the kitchen, she was just putting the finishing touches to the cake.

The minute that Rose saw Tom she rushed over to him and said: "Oh Tom, Mary's dead." With that, all resolve for composure went out of the window and Rose once again started to sob. Between great gulps of air, she managed to tell Tom what had happened.

"Poor love," Tom said as he held Rose tightly to his chest and stroked her hair. Ben leaned against Tom's legs, nudging him for attention and for a while the three of them just stood there in silence other than the odd sniff from Rose. Finally, she pulled away from Tom and put on the kettle for some tea. Just then the phone rang, and Tom answered it. As he concluded the conversation he turned to Rose and said, "What's this about collecting Puff?"

Rose bit her lip and said very quietly, "I told Susan that we would look after Puff."

"But what about Ben? How will he feel about us taking in another dog?"

"Oh, Ben will be fine, Tom. Puff is a very friendly dog. He's got some Lab in him. He's a cross between a Labrador and a Golden Retriever. Look, if Ben is too put out by him, I'll look for another home for Puff. But I just know that Mary would have wanted me to look after her beloved dog. Can't you see that?"

"Yes, I suppose so my darling. Anyway, you had better go around to pick up the dog. We'll just have to see how Ben reacts to another dog on his turf."

Mary lived on Christy Street. Rose drove there quickly and parked in front of the small cottage that had been her friend's house. She had spent many hours visiting Mary for coffee over the past year, so Rose was quite familiar with the home. An O.P.P car was parked in the driveway.

Rose knocked on the door which was opened by a handsome and incredibly young-looking officer. He looked vaguely familiar to Rose.

"You must be Rose Blair?" He said. "I'm Constable Elliot, please come in. The dog is in the kitchen."

"Have I met you somewhere before, Constable?" Rose asked as she followed him into the house.

"Oh. Yes, ma'am. I spoke to you at the cemetery earlier today."

Rose nodded as she remembered his kind face as he had told her that she could go home. *I must have looked a real mess,* she thought, recalling her tears.

It seemed odd to be walking through Mary's house without her cheerful voice chatting away. Rose walked past the living room and into the kitchen which was at the back of the house.

Looking around as if for the first time, she realized that there was a distinct absence of photographs anywhere. Compared to Rose's house where they had photographs all over the place, Mary's home seemed strangely devoid of anything personal.

Odd, Rose thought, she had known that her friend was extremely private, but it had never before struck her as strange that there was absolutely no evidence of her past life.

Puff was lying in his dog basket, his golden head resting between his shaggy paws.

"He knows that Mary is dead," Rose said to Constable Elliot. "He just knows."

She collected his dog bowl and clipped on his leash.

"Come on, Puff, let's go home to Ben."

TWO

Susan managed to secure the Lion's Hall and set it up for their Incident Room. She had contacted the Serious Crimes Unit in London and had requested that Constable Mathieson and Sergeant Flowers be seconded to Bayfield for the duration of their enquiries.

Both officers had proven to be invaluable the previous year when solving the murder on Bayfield beach. They had worked well together as a team and that, thought Susan, was the main criteria for success. Constables Elliot and Brown were also seconded to Bayfield for two weeks only.

With the Incident Room ready all that was needed were some accommodations. The previous year Susan had stayed firstly at The Cottage Colony, then after Jim Reynolds disappearance, she had moved into The Bayfield Village Inn.

She enjoyed swimming in their lovely indoor pool. That would be her first choice of accommodation. An hour later she was checked in at the Inn and was back at The Lion's Hall ready for the two o'clock briefing with her team.

Susan booted up her computer and downloaded the photographs

taken of the body at the scene of the crime. Four officers were seated around the huge table presumably used for Lion's meetings. Once again Susan was shocked by how young and fresh faced they looked, *could be high school kids if it wasn't for their uniforms*, Susan thought as she stood up to address the team.

"Good afternoon everyone. I think I know all of you, but I believe Constable Elliot and Brown you haven't met Sergeant Flowers or Constable Mathieson. We all worked together last year on the murder of three people. The perpetrator is still at large in Europe and last seen in Vienna. Interpol is still on the case.

Now listen up, the body of a woman was found brutally murdered in the cemetery just outside of the village. Her name was Mary Stokes. She was found by her friend Rose Blair. The two women were meeting to practice for their game of croquet.

Susan picked up some photographs from the table and proceeded to pass them around.

"The croquet club borders onto the cemetery. From the way the body was slumped over the headstone, plus the piece of white material left on the fence, implies that Mary Stokes was trying to flee from her killer. As you can see from these photographs, she was killed by a crossbow shooting a deadly arrow. Sergeant Flowers, I would like you to research everything there is to know about crossbows. See if there are any archery clubs around here and try to find out where one can purchase a crossbow. Forensics will let us know the actual specifics of her death but seemingly she was shot through the chest with such force that she was actually impaled to the headstone. No sign of struggle, no sexual assault, just a cold-hearted planned execution style killing.

Turning to the young Constable Susan continued to give out her instructions.

"Constable Mathieson, find out all you can about our victim. It appears that she moved to Bayfield from Guelph about one year ago. Find and interview anyone who knew her, and there was an ex-husband, find him too. Constables Brown and Elliot, you are to inter-view all the locals. Ask if they have seen anyone out of the ordinary or witnessed anyone hunting with a crossbow. Also, ask around about Mary Stokes. Was she well liked in the community? At the moment we know very little about her. Right everyone, let's meet again tomorrow morning, 8 o'clock sharp."

Susan glanced at the clock on the wall. It was only 3:00pm, too early for dinner. She suddenly felt ravenous. She had skipped lunch although she had eaten some scones at Rose's house. Thinking about food triggered her appetite.

She decided to walk to DaVinci's where she could get herself a cup of coffee and a sandwich.

Bayfield Main Street was buzzing with people, mostly women shopping. August in Bayfield was always busy. Susan walked to DaVinci's past the counter and through to the back of the restaurant and onto the patio.

A pretty woman sitting at the adjacent table directed her gaze at Susan.

"Aren't you the detective who was here last year for the murder enquiry?"

"Um...yes, and you are?" Susan said impatiently as she looked around for the waitress to take her order.

"I'm Lena. You interviewed me. I volunteer for the Historical Society in the Archives room. Remember the map of the shipwrecks of the Great Storm of 1913? Well, I put that together. Are you here because of that awful murder at the Croquet Club?"

How fast bad news travels, Susan thought as she ordered her coffee and sandwich. She answered Lena politely, "Yes, I am. Did you know Mary Stokes?"

"Only in passing. Rose Blair was her best friend. Mind you, she had only been living in the village for a year. It's so awful."

"Had you seen her recently with anyone other than Rose?" Susan asked.

"Well, actually, yes. A few days ago she was sitting out here having coffee with a man. They appeared to be deep in conversation, not arguing as such, but a heated discussion was certainly taking place. Mary left quite abruptly if I remember right."

The waitress interrupted their conversation asking if Susan was ready to place her order. Having requested a large coffee and a ham sandwich, Susan turned back to Lena and continued her questioning.

"Could you describe the man to me, Lena?"

"Oh, now you're asking. Well... he was in his fifties or sixties, heavy built with thin, greying hair, no real distinguishing features other than what he was wearing which was a very loud, red plaid shirt. Sorry I can't be more explicit."

"You've been a great help. Right, I must be off. See you around Lena and thank you for your help."

Susan paid for her coffee and sandwich and walked back to the Lion's Hall. As she passed The Black Dog memories of the previous year and her relationship with Jim Reynolds came flooding back. The Black Dog had been their favourite restaurant.

She hurried by and walked past The Albion, around the corner past Brandon's Hardware, and The Spa until she reached The Lion's Hall where she had left her car. Susan looked at her watch. It was just 4:00pm.

Time enough to go back to The Bayfield Village Inn, go for a swim and change for dinner at The Docks and then an early night so that she could face the next day with a completely fresh mind.

BEN WASN'T sure what to make of Puff. He wanted to play with the dog, yet all Puff did was sit by the front door as if waiting for his mistress to return.

Rose and Tom had tried to coax him over to the sun lounge, to even sit on the sofa with them, but for the last day, apart from eating a bowl of food, he had stubbornly remained posted at the front door.

Rose wondered if Puff knew that Mary was dead. Dogs were intuitive, maybe he just sensed that she wasn't coming back but how long would he just sit there and wait?

Over breakfast Tom asked Rose about Mary.

"You said that you think that she was married before, love? Surely she must have talked to you about it?"

"Oh Tom, you never knew Mary. She was very private, and I never liked to intrude on her privacy. I always felt that if she wanted to tell me about her past she would but in her own time. She did once say something about her first love and when I asked about it, she just clammed up.

You know there were no photographs in her house, in fact, I hadn't realized how impersonal her place was until I went around to pick up Puff. Somehow when Mary was around it didn't matter.

Her house seemed to warm and lit up by her very presence. Tom, she was a lovely woman and I miss her already." Rose felt tears well up in her eyes and she blew her nose hard.

"Well, love, the police will piece it all together but if you say that she was lovely then she surely must have been. But if she was married before her ex-husband must be around somewhere. I presume there were no children?"

"I honestly don't know, Tom. Once when I was at her house we were discussing a book that we had both read. Mary was busy making coffee in the kitchen and she asked if I could fetch the book from her bedside. I remember going into her room and seeing a framed photograph at the side of her bed. The picture showed a handsome man in his thirties with his arms around a young Mary. There were two young children standing in front of their parents. When I asked Mary about the photograph she said that it was her sister and family but I'm not so sure now."

"But Rose, why would she deliberately lie to you? That's what I don't understand. Oh well, let's leave it to the police to find out. Now, what time is Jessica arriving with those two little monkeys Abby and Ella?"

Jessica had phoned to say that Rob and she would be dropping the girls off early evening before they headed out to Toronto. Rose had two hours to prepare for their darling grandchildren.

The spaghetti pie and chocolate cake were already baked. Tom had made up the beds. In fact, there was nothing more to be done so Rose suggested that they took the dogs for a walk.

"I do hope that Puff is good with the children. He's not used to them." Rose fretted while getting ready to go out.

"Don't worry, love. It might just be the best thing for him being distracted by Abby and Ella. Come on Ben, let's put on your leash."

Ben came galloping across the hall, exuberant as ever, excited by the prospect of a walk. Puff docilely let Rose clip on his leash and off they went down Bayfield Terrace to Long Hill.

Tom was just pointing out a large, new, forty-foot boat moored next to their own boat, *Tranquility*, when Puff, who had been very subdued, let out a loud bark.

Rose and Tom looked up and to their horror saw a big, black Mercedes heading straight towards them at an alarming speed.

Tom pushed Rose and the dogs into the ditch just as the car swerved into them. Neither of them had time to collect their senses when they saw the big Mercedes do a three-point turn and head back towards them again.

"Rose, jump," Tom yelled and just in time they both ended up in the ditch again, yet this time the threatening vehicle drove off.

"Tom, Tom, did you get the license number?" Rose cried while brushing off some twigs and dirt from her blouse.

"Yes, I'll never forget it. Now quick, we must get home and call the police."

Neither of them had brought their cell phones with them.

Afterward, in the safety of their living room, Rose realized that it had been Puff who had saved them. If he hadn't had alerted them with his bark, then they would never have been warned in time. But who would want to harm them and why?

"Tom, I'm frightened," Rose said softly as she put the kettle on for a cup of tea.

"Don't worry, darling, the police are coming over. They'll get to the bottom of all of this, well, at least I can give them the license plate number."

Ten minutes later there was a knock on the door. Tom opened it and there stood Inspector Susan Parker.

"Gosh, that was quick. Rose," he called, "Susan Parker is here."

Tom looked away from Susan hoping that his embarrassment would not show on his face. After the previous year's indiscretion, he had not been able to look the Inspector in the eyes without cringing. He thought that he had managed to forget that kiss but somehow, every now and then, he had guiltily relived the moment.

"Susan, I'm so glad you came so quickly. Tom and I have been quite frightened by what happened."

Rose continued to relay the whole story and Tom finally inter-jected with the license plate number.

"Oh, and yesterday, early in the morning, I found Ben outside in the garden and the back door open. I don't know if there is any connection but we're definitely feeling worried."

Susan looked thoughtful.

"I don't believe in coincidences and right now there are just too many for my liking. Look, don't you worry. I'll get our team onto this. My advice to you is to make sure that you lock the house very securely and that you keep your eyes and ears open. I'm so sorry that you have to deal with all of this now, particularly after the shock of your friend's death. "

"Thanks Susan. You really must come around for a proper social visit, maybe dinner sometime. This weekend we have Abby and Ella staying here but we'll try for one day next week. I'll call you. Bye."

Susan left and before Tom and Rose had time to talk Jessica and

Rob pulled into their driveway. The back door of their car burst open and Abby and Ella came running out like two little whirlwinds.

"Grandma, Grandpa, we're spending the weekend with you. Where's Ben?"

At the sound of his name Ben came padding out followed tentatively by Puff.

"Girls," Rose said. "We have a new dog. His name is Puff and he is very shy. You must be especially kind to him because he is a little unsure of us and we want him to feel at home."

"Grandma, Puff is funny looking," squealed Ella. "He's got a funny face and fluffy, pointy ears. Come here, Puff."

Puff sat down and let out a big sigh. Abby and Ella rushed over and started talking to him and stroked his shaggy head.

"Nice Puffy, nice Puffy, you and Ben will be best of friends. We love you Puffy."

Jessica and Rob kissed the girls goodbye and quickly left. They had a long journey ahead of them to get to Toronto.

THREE

The team was all gathered at the Lion's Hall. The smell of coffee hung in the air as Susan called her group together.

"Now listen up everyone. Let's have the reports first. Sergeant Flowers, what have you to report?"

"Well, ma'am, there's not much online about our victim, Mary Stokes. The trouble is she has quite a common name. It took some digging to unearth the little that I've got. I started in Guelph and found that she had been married from 1998 until 2007. Mary's ex-husbands name is Graham Stokes.

I have a contact number and address for this Graham Stokes and with your permission, ma'am, I was going to drive up to Guelph after this meeting today to check him out. "

"Thank you, Sergeant. Now, Constables Brown and Elliot, what have you found out from the local people of Bayfield?"

"Not a lot, ma'am. It appears that our victim was a very private person. Other than Rose Blair, she seemed to have few friends. Everyone we spoke to said that she was always smiling and very polite. The librarian seemed to think that she had no family in this area or indeed anywhere for that matter. It seems that she paid her bills on time and was always friendly and polite, but other than that nobody seems to know much about her. I'll keep digging, ma'am."

The Sergeant put his notebook away.

"Thank you, both. Actually, I have something else to add to our Mary Stokes dossier. I was talking to Lena from the Historical Society and she mentioned that a few days ago she saw Mary having a heated conversation with a man over coffee at DaVinci's. He was apparently in his 50's, thinning grey hair, nothing very distinguishable other than the bright red plaid shirt that he was wearing.

So, Constable Elliot, your job is to find more about this man. Constable Brown keep asking the locals, and also, I suggest, talk to some of the ladies at the fitness class. They meet Mondays, Wednesdays, and Fridays from 9 to 10am at the arena. Ok, who have we got left? Oh, Constable Mathieson, any news on the crossbow archery clubs in this area?"

Constable Mathieson pulled out his notebook.

"Yes, ma'am, you can purchase all archery equipment including crossbows and arrows, from the Huron Sports Outfitters in Kippen, also from Canadian Tire and TSC in Goderich. I've set up a meeting with a local hunter who is going to show me the different crossbows and talk me through how they work. I'll be seeing him tomorrow. That's all I have to report right now, ma'am."

"Thank you, Constable. Now listen up everyone. So far, we have very little information to go on. Our victim, Mary Stokes, age 56, seems to be a bit of an enigma. One year in the village and she seems to have made friends with just one person, Rose Blair.

She did, however, join the fitness class and, presumably, the Croquet Club. She was married for nine years to one Graham Stokes of Guelph. The other piece of information is that she was seen arguing with a middle-aged man wearing a bright red shirt.

So far, gentlemen, we have very little to go on, very little indeed.

We need to know much more about our Mary Stokes and find out why someone wanted her dead. Go to it men and bring me some information. Same time tomorrow morning."

The men shuffled their papers together and got ready to leave. Susan called Sergeant Flowers over.

"Sergeant, I think that I would like to accompany you to Guelph to interview Graham Stokes. Should I drive or do you want to?"

"I like driving, ma'am. Is there anything that you need to do before we leave, or shall we go now?"

"No, let's go now and hopefully we'll be back by mid-afternoon and miss the end of the day traffic."

They set off straight away and drove past Varna, Brucefield, and on to Seaforth, where they went straight across at the traffic lights and drove until they reached Winthrop Line. They turned right and drove until they got to Phillipsburg and joined up with the New Hamburg road to Kitchener then onto the 401. It took them a little over two hours to reach Guelph. Graham Stokes lived on the south side of the city, close to the Sleeman's brewery.

"So, what does Mr. Stokes do for a living?" Susan asked as they pulled into the driveway of a modest split ranch house. A beat-up old Chevrolet sat in the driveway. The house had a general air of neglect hanging over it.

"He was a custodian of St. Vincent's School here in Guelph. He lost his job about the same time as Mary walked out of their marriage. I believe that alcohol was involved."

Susan knocked on the door and stood back when it was opened by a heavy-set man with a thick, bushy beard, sporting tattoos laced down his arms. *Biker* came immediately to mind as Susan showed him her badge and asked if they could come in.

Graham Stokes proved not to be difficult at all. His outward appearance belied the fact that he was a broken man. His story was as typical as many other marriage break-ups caused by alcoholism.

He had met Mary at the school, St. Vincent's, where he was the custodian and she was the school secretary. Over a period of two years, they had dated and then married in 1997.

They had no children together although he had a son by his first marriage, George, whom he had not seen for ten years.

When he was asked if Mary had any other family Graham's face clouded over as he said, "She was such a private person; you know she never talked about her family. When I asked, she said that she had no family at all and left it at that. She did try to be a good stepmother to George who was sixteen at the time of our marriage, but no one could get through to George. He was a rebel. Into drugs and alcohol. He even spent time at The Blue Water Youth Correctional Centre."

Susan interrupted Graham. "Where does your ex-wife live now and does George keep in touch with you?"

"Jean, my ex, lives just outside of Exeter in a small village called Hensall. Yes, George often stays with his mother, well, at least he used to, but I haven't a clue if he is still in contact. As to me... well, he used to only contact me when he needed money but, as I said before, I haven't seen him for years."

"Could we have her contact address and telephone number, please?"

Graham wrote out the necessary information. Susan and Sergeant Flowers left Guelph, driving down the 401, feeling as if they had at last made a bit of headway with their enquiries. They still knew very little about Mary Stokes but at least her life was beginning to unravel in small threads and soon they would be able to weave it all together to get a complete picture of sorts.

"ABBY, Ella, are you ready? I'm going in five minutes. Leave Puff and Ben alone. You can play with them when we get back."

Rose had decided to take the girls to the Splash Pad and then treat them to an ice cream afterwards.

It was another beautiful August morning. The sky was an azure blue and a gentle breeze stirred the air. Tom had planned to go sailing while Rose took the children to the park.

"Grandma, can't we take Puff with us to the Splash Pad?" Abby plaintively asked. Both girls had fallen in love with Puff who now seemed a changed dog. No longer depressed and subdued, he reveled in their attention and seemed to soak it up like a sponge.

"No, darling, we can't take dogs onto the Splash Pad. He might frighten some of the children. Puff will be fine staying here with Ben. Right... are you both ready?"

They walked down Louisa Street to Clan Gregor Square, where several families were having picnics in the park and the Splash Pad was fairly teeming with kids.

Rose parked herself on one of the benches and helped Abby and Ella remove their 'T' shirts and shorts. Abby, pretty in pink with everything coordinated including her frilly pink ankle socks.

Ella, in sharp contrast, wore a jumble of colours and a pair of flip-flops.

Soon they were running in front of the jets of water and having a great time splashing each other. Rose looked around at the other people enjoying the park and Splash Pad.

Many were cottagers, people on holiday, but there were a few other grannies like herself with their grandchildren who Rose knew from her fitness class.

She was just waving at one such woman when out of the corner of her eye she saw a black Mercedes cruising down the road by the Town Hall. It looked just like the car that had deliberately tried to run them over.

She stood up to try to get a better view of the license plate and sure enough, she realized with a jolt, it was the same registration. Rose felt her heart miss a beat.

"Abby, Ella, quick, come here my darlings. We have to go home now."

"Oh, but Grandma, can't we stay longer? You promised us ice cream."

"Yes, my darlings, but Grandma needs you to get home now. Hurry up, please."

Abby and Ella reluctantly trudged over to where Rose was standing. She was scanning the cars parked around the Square. Why hadn't she taken Tom's advice a year ago when he offered to get her an I-phone and she had flatly refused the offer, saying that it would just be a waste of their money as why would she need a cell phone in Bayfield?

She suddenly realized that the Lions Hall was literally just across the road. Inspector Parker and her team would be there, and they could try to intersect the black Mercedes. Taking the girls hands Rose almost ran across the road with Abby and Ella squealing by her side.

"Sorry, my darlings, but Grandma needs to talk to the police quickly. Look, we're almost there now."

They had reached the Lion's Hall. Rose could see Inspector Parker sitting with her team around a long conference table. She suddenly felt awkward interrupting their meeting. She knocked on the door tentatively.

"Come in," called a voice that Rose did not recognize.

Abby, Ella, and Rose entered the room which would normally be very familiar to Rose as the Historical Society held their monthly meetings in the same room. It was all business now with policemen sitting around and flip charts with diagrams and then, to Rose's horror, photographs of her dear friend Mary pinned onto the wall.

She quickly stepped out of the room with the girls at her side hoping that their little eyes had not seen the dreadful photographs. Susan Parker came over and said, "Is everything alright Rose?"

"Well, actually it isn't. We were at the Splash Pad when I saw the black Mercedes again, you know the one that tried to run us down. It's back in the village, Susan, and I'm terrified of what it might do.

We've got the girls staying with us for the weekend and Tom is off sailing. Oh, I'm so sorry to disturb you. I probably sound a bit hysterical..."

"No, Rose, you did the right thing coming here. Look, I'll get Sergeant Flowers to run the girls and yourself home and he can check that everything's ok. Here, I'll dispatch an alert out to all O.P.P cruisers in the county. Don't worry. We'll get to the bottom of this."

Sergeant Flowers came out and with great squeals of delight Abby and Ella climbed into the cruiser. Rose had never ridden in a Police car before and was amazed at all the electronics on the dashboard. It was just like being part of a movie, although this was no cop show but the real thing.

They drove down Charles Street, crossing Howard and turning right where they crossed the Main Street, and drove up to Colina. Here they took a right turn onto Louisa and finally, a left onto Bayfield Terrace.

As the Constable parked his car and the girls and Rose got out, they could hear both dogs barking. *Puff must be feeling better,* Rose thought as they entered the house and the two dogs came bounding out to greet them.

"I'll just go inside ahead of you, Mrs. Blair, and check everything out," Sergeant Flowers said as Abby and Ella threw their chubby arms around Puff and Ben, tails wagging, dancing around Rose.

"Yes, thank you Sergeant, we'll be in shortly." Rose said as she untangled herself from almost being tripped up by Ben. "Come on Abby and Ella, let's go inside and get some lemonade and cookies."

"But grandma, you promised us ice cream," wailed Abby as she not so gently pulled Puff towards the front door.

"Well, I'll set out two bowls of ice cream for you two in the sunroom, but first we need to go and wash your hands. Come on Ben, Puff, in you come."

Sergeant Flowers appeared and gave the "all clear" to Rose. He promised to send a cruiser around to check on the neighbourhood and with that he departed leaving Rose to scoop out ice cream while still deep in thought.

FOUR

Good morning everyone." Susan shuffled her papers around and pulled out the piece she was looking for. "I have here a copy of the preliminary forensics report. Our victim was killed by a twelve-inch, titanium arrow which shot her through her main ventricle at a speed of 70mph causing major internal hemorrhaging. Death would have been almost instantaneous. Titanium arrows, Constable Mathieson, you said that there was a shop in Kippen that sold all manner of hunting gear. Go back and check whether they sell titanium arrows. I suspect that they are rare, anything made from titanium is usually expensive."

Susan paused before continuing.

"We know the means, but so far a motive had eluded us. Sergeant Flowers and I interviewed Mary Stokes' husband, Graham Stokes. He has a son, George, who now lives with his mother somewhere between Hensall and Exeter. This son has a record, nothing serious mind you, but he did do a stint at the Blue Water Correctional centre when it was still open. Sergeant Flowers is going to follow up with this inquiry this afternoon. Right. Constables Elliot and Brown, anymore from the locals of Bayfield? Did you talk to any of the Fitness Class ladies? We still don't know much about Mary Stokes."

Constable Elliot stood up and pulled out his notebook. Flipping through the pages he started to speak hesitantly, clearly not at ease in a group.

"Um... well, everybody said that Mary Stokes was a lovely person. Only two of the ladies interviewed had been to her home and one of those was Rose Blair who we already know. The other lady, Linda Walsh, had been to Mary's for coffee a couple of times. She, too, said how lovely she was but also how private. I asked if Mary had any family and Linda said that she was evasive when talking about her past. She had mentioned something about an ex in Guelph. She also said that Mary had lost her parents over twenty years ago. That is all I have to add, ma'am."

"Thank you, Constable Elliot. Now, Constable Mathieson, I would like you to gather as much information as you can about the Croquet Club. Also, find out who was playing croquet the same morning as Rose and Mary were scheduled to play. Someone knew that the ladies were going to be there at that time of day.

Sergeant Flowers, did you have any joy in tracking down that Black Mercedes?"

Sergeant Flowers stood up and said:

"Well, ma'am, the vehicles license plate led us nowhere. It was registered to a numbered company and when I checked out the owners of the said company, I found that it did not actually exist anymore. I'll keep digging. One thing I did establish is that the vehicle had originally been purchased in Quebec."

"Thank you, Sergeant. So, it appears that the black Mercedes is definitely under suspicion but what is the connection, if there is a connection, to our victim and why have the Blair's been singled out? Keep probing, Sergeant Flowers, I know that there will be a reason for this threatening behaviour. Keep up the surveillance of the Blair property and keep your eyes open for that black Mercedes.

Now, Constable, I will accompany you this afternoon to interview Jean and George Stokes. The rest of you, bring me something to work on, we need a break. Go to it everyone. Report back here tomorrow, same time."

The officers shuffled their papers and ambled out of the Lion's Hall. Susan stood back and called over to Constable Mathieson.

"Constable, I would like us to stop by the Huron Sports Shop in Kippen. Can you telephone Jean Stokes and confirm our meeting. Also check to see if George will be around. We do need to interview him as well. Ok, go and get some lunch and we'll meet back here in one hour."

Susan left the Constable to his phone call. She decided to go to the Thai restaurant for her lunch.

Walking across Clan Gregor Square Susan surveyed the park and the Main Street to the west of the Square. It was such a beautiful village. She always felt so relaxed when being in Bayfield and part of the community. *To live here would be so good for my soul*, she thought as she crossed the highway.

The Thai restaurant had a small patio to the rear of the building and that is where Susan headed. She walked through the inside of the restaurant which was beautifully decorated with teak carvings on the wall and little orchids on each table. The owner was from Thailand and cooked amazing food.

Susan sat outside under an umbrella, little water fountains tinkling in the background. She was soon served and devoured a wonderful plate full of Pad Thai washed down with a Speckled Hen beer.

She looked at her watch. There still was twenty minutes to kill before she was to meet back at the Lion's Hall. She would walk to the pharmacy around the corner on the Highway and purchase some Advil for the dull headache that she had woken up with that morning.

It would also be a good opportunity to speak to the staff at the pharmacy about Mary Stokes.

She was greeted warmly by the pharmacist's assistant who found her the well needed Advil. Susan paid for them and then introduced herself as a police officer showing her badge before asking any questions.

"I am investigating the murder of Mary Stokes. Was she one of your patients?"

The young man went to the computer and typed in her name.

"Yes, she had a repeat prescription from us which she picked up every two months.

"Could you tell me what she had been prescribed?"

Susan was waiting for the usual response about patient confidentiality but was pleasantly surprised when the young man volunteered the information willingly.

"Well, Inspector, the poor lady is dead and so confidentiality is no longer an issue. I can tell you that she was taking Clonazepam, a benzodiazepine drug having anxiolytic muscle relaxant, sedative, and hypnotic properties, really a sedative to relieve anxiety. She was suffering from depression."

"Thank you. You have been most helpful. Would you mind printing off a copy of this prescription for me, please?"

Susan left the Pharmacy in deep thought. So Mary was suffering from depression. Could that have any bearing on her death, Susan pondered whilst walking to the Lion's Hall past the Town Hall. Of course, being depressed could have nothing to do with her murder, she had rationalized by the time that she reached the Lion's Hall.

Children were shrieking with delight over at the Splash pad where a large number of mums and grandmas sat on benches watching their young children enjoy themselves.

Constable Mathieson was waiting inside his car. The two of them were on the road by 1:00pm sharp.

· · ·

AFTER A BREAKFAST of pancakes and maple syrup Rose decided to take the girls to the Dollar Store in Goderich. This had become a treat which was almost part of a ritual of their stay whenever they visited. Tom would give them some 'pocket money' to spend in the store and Rose would give twenty minutes to choose 'wisely' what to spend their money on.

Rose also wanted to visit the supermarket to buy some more Kibbles. Puff had suddenly regained his appetite and was eating them out of house and home.

Thinking of Puff and his complete about turn, Rose smiled. It appeared that the dog had finished his period of mourning and was now absolutely besotted with Abby and Ella.

Fickle creature, she thought with a laugh, yet it was the resilience of nature that kept all animals going Rose pondered as she rounded up the girls and buckled them up in their seats in the car.

Tom was going to play golf with Doug and would not be back before lunch.

"Right. Off we go to Goderich. Dollar Store here we come!"

Rose drove onto the highway and over the bridge where she turned right down Old River Road.

At the stop sign, before crossing over to Carriage Lane, Rose looked towards where her friend Sheila lived. She would give her a call later on that day when they got home from shopping.

She wondered if Sheila even knew about Mary as she had been away. Sheila, Mary, and Rose would get together every now and then and have coffee together and Rose knew that Sheila would be truly shocked by the news of her friend's death.

Rose turned right off Carriage Lane, onto Bayfield River Road, then turned left at Orchard Line. She drove past the Berry Farm which sold the most divine fruit pies and other baked goodies and ten minutes later the car was parked outside the Dollar Store. Abby and Ella charged into the store ahead of Rose who called out to them to wait for Grandma.

Abby chose a bead making set and Ella chose a Cinderella jigsaw puzzle. It only took the girls ten minutes which, Rose thought, was something of a record.

They had just paid for their goods and were about to get in the car, when Rose looked up and saw in the Tim Horton's car park, a black Mercedes. A man with a dark beard, short in stature, swarthy in appearance, was preoccupied with his cell phone.

Rose hurried the girls into the car and, with her heart beating like a drum, she drove quickly out of the car park. Just as she approached the main road the man put his cell phone away and jumped into his car.

Rose made a snap decision. If he was following her, she did not want to be alone with him on a country road like Orchard Line. She would be safer driving back to Bayfield along Highway 21 where she could drive into the O.P.P station just five kilometres out of Goderich.

She drove down Sun Coast Drive and took a left at the traffic lights opposite the McDonalds. Once again Rose wished that she had listened to Tom and had got a cell phone. She definitely would take him up on his offer now.

Pulling into the O.P.P station a few minutes later Rose quickly unbuckled Abby and Ella and told them to follow her. All the time she scanned the Highway for the black Mercedes. Just as she opened the door of the O.P.P building she saw the Mercedes slow down.

Again, she managed to get a really good look at the driver. Her overall impression was that he looked definitely foreign, possibly Middle Eastern. His face would be etched into her memory for a long time yet to come.

Rose explained to the policeman at the desk her predicament and gave him the description of the driver as well as the license plate numbers. She explained that the Bayfield Police team were onto the case too.

The O.P.P officer said that he would dispatch a cruiser straight away and they would contact Bayfield and suggest that they put out a surveillance team around Rose's property.

It was almost lunch time by the time they finally got home. Jessica and Rob were due to pick the girls up sometime around 2:00pm.

Tom and Doug were sitting in The Albion having a pint of beer each. It had been pretty hot out on the golf course and each contemplated their game while enjoying their cold beer.

The Albion was busy. In one corner a group of journalists, including a camera man and sound technician, were interviewing the owner. An animated discussion seemed to be taking place and Tom recognized the interviewer, Sophia, from the local news channel CTV 2 in London.

She was an attractive dark-haired brunette with almond shaped eyes and as he was taking in the scene she looked over and caught Tom's eye. At that point the owner turned round and gestured over to Doug and Tom.

Tom quickly looked back at his drink but too late, Sophia was making her way over followed by the crew. She stopped in front of Doug and Tom and said,

"Which of you is Tom Blair?" Tom nodded and then she said, "Would you mind if I ask you a few questions?"

Tom had never been interviewed on television before and felt acutely embarrassed. He nodded gamely and she ploughed on.

"I understand that it was your wife that found the body?"

Tom wasn't sure how much he should say but he mumbled, "Yes".

Sophia continued.

"So, the murder took place at the Croquet Club?"

Tom spoke up because if there was one thing he disliked and that was misinformation. "Well, actually, Mary was found dead in the cemetery, not the Croquet Club."

Sophia persisted, "But she was playing Croquet, wasn't she?"

"Yes, Rose and Mary had a game booked for 9:00 a.m. that morning. They had gone to the courts early to practice."

'So, Mary Stokes was a friend of your wife's?"

"Yes, a good friend. Now I really must be getting home."

With that Tom and Doug finished their drink and got up to leave. As they were leaving Sophia ran after them saying,

"Do you have any idea who would have committed this dreadful murder?"

He refused to say anything else and drove off as fast as he could just hoping that the news crew would not follow him.

Tom was home when Rose pulled up to the driveway.

"Grandpa, we went to the Dollar Store and look what I bought," Abby explained completely oblivious to the stress that Rose had been put through earlier.

"Oh Grandpa, we stopped at the Police Station and talked to a nice man in a uniform." Ella said while pulling out her jigsaw puzzle and opening the box.

"Come on, girls, let's go through to the sunroom. I'll get us some lunch while you play with your purchases."

Rose caught Tom's eye and nodded towards the kitchen. Soon the girls were engrossed playing with Puff and Ben which gave Rose the opportunity to talk to Tom. She told him about the black Mercedes and the rather sinister looking driver.

"Tom, just who is he and why is he following us?"

"I don't know love, but I mean to find out. I don't want to worry you, but the press was on to me at the Albion. That Sophia, you know the news gal from the London newsroom, well she was there with a camera man and sound man interviewing the owner of the pub. Talk about persistent."

Rose, as usual when stressed decided to bake and let Tom play with the girls in the sunroom while she made a rhubarb custard pie especially for Jessica who had claimed the pie to be her favourite right from the tender age of two.

. . .

SERGEANT FLOWERS and Susan pulled up outside a run down, single story bungalow with paint peeling off the front door and windows and siding that looked as if it hadn't seen paint in years. Jean Stokes had agreed to meet them at her house, but she wasn't sure if her son, George, would turn up or not.

They knocked on the front door. It was opened by a tired looking woman who must have been in her fifties. She had shoulder length stringy, dyed brown hair which badly needed a trim. Her face was lined and care worn although her eyes showed a level of intelligence and sparkle at odds with her face.

"Good afternoon, Mrs. Stokes. This is Sergeant Flowers, and I am Inspector Parker. Could we come in?"

They were shown into a comfortable if worn living room. The television was on, "Today's Show" with Matt Lauer chatting away. Jean Stokes turned to Susan and said, "So how can I help you? What has George done now?"

"Mrs. Stokes, we are not here to discuss your son although we would like to speak to him. No, the reason for our visit is that we are trying to gather information about Mary Stokes. I believe that George spent some time living with his father when Mary and he were still together. Is there anything that you can tell us about her?"

"Oh, you're here because of that murder in Bayfield. I must say that it came as a mighty shock when I heard about it on the radio. I quite liked her you know."

The kitchen door opened and a man with thin, grey hair walked into the room.

"Joseph, this is Inspector Parker and Sergeant Flowers.

They're here to talk about that poor woman, Mary, who was murdered a few days ago in Bayfield."

Susan looked at Joseph intently. *Could this be the same man that*

Lena had described as having a heated argument with Mary at DaVinci's? She wondered.

"Um... Mr...Joseph, do you by any chance own a bright red, plaid shirt?"

Joseph looked taken aback but before he could answer Susan, Jean smiled and said.

"Oh, that ugly thing. Yes, he has a red, plaid shirt which I hate him wearing."

"Joseph, you were seen having a heated discussion with Mary Stokes only a few weeks ago at DaVinci's in Bayfield. Could you tell us what the discussion was about? Would you mind if we take a statement from you?"

Joseph looked uncomfortable and clearly Jean was intrigued to find out.

"If you must know it was about George. You see Mary had been sending him money and I wanted her to stop. He just used her money to feed his habit. Jean's son is into crystal meth. He's been in and out of rehab and just when he seems to be turning a corner and getting clean, he goes back on it again.

I swear that it was only because of the money that Mary sent to him. I met with her to ask if she would stop funding his habit."

"What did Mary say to you when you accused her of supporting his drug abuse?"

"Well, she was very defensive. She said that she only sent him the odd $20 note and that wouldn't be enough to feed his habit. She told me to mind my own business and not to interfere in other people's lives."

"Thank you, Joseph. I presume that you are Jean's husband or partner?"

"We've never got married but we're common law, been together for ten years, haven't we Jean?"

Jean rolled her eyes but smiled.

"Yes, you old fool. Inspector, this man has been like a saint dealing with George and all the problems that we've had with him. I couldn't have managed without him."

"Was George close to Mary?"

"Not really. In the early years after I split with Graham, he used to spend the odd weekend in Guelph with his dad and when Mary came along, she treated him well, but he was in and out of the Blue Water Youth Correctional so many times nothing anyone could have done would have changed the outcome. It was the drugs you see, always the drugs."

Susan looked at Jean and marveled at the sanity of the woman. First, she had to deal with an alcoholic husband and then years of a wayward son ruining his life on drugs. *Poor woman,* Susan thought. *What an awful burden to bear.*

"Is George around then?" Sergeant Flowers said.

"He's gone hunting with his mates." Joseph said gruffly.

"What sort of hunting, Joseph?" Susan asked.

"Well, he had his rifle taken away from him. No license. So now he uses the crossbow more often than not."

Both Susan and Sergeant Flowers went very quiet.

"You said a crossbow? Could you check and see if he's taken his bow with him?"

"He doesn't keep his gear here anymore. It's all around at his friend Tyler's place. But they're probably out hunting now. I can give you his address if you like?"

Joseph got out some paper and a pen and proceeded to write. When he was finished, he handed it over to Susan.

"Thank you, Joseph. One more thing, Jean. Did you ever hear Mary talk about her family? We are trying to trace any relatives but so far we have drawn a blank."

Jean thought for a while before replying.

"She was a dark horse, that one. When I first met her on a weekend, I was dropping off George to stay with his dad, we had a long chat about this and that.

I remember asking her about her family. She became very quiet and looked so sad.

She never actually answered my question, but my sense was one of loss. She looked haunted to me. There was an air of melancholy about her, especially back then."

"Well, thank you to both of you. You've been most helpful. We're obviously not going to get to see George today, but we will be back to interview him, if you could relay that to him."

With that they departed both deep in thought.

THE HOUSE WAS BLISSFULLY QUIET. Abby and Ella had left with their parents at 4:00 pm and Tom had insisted that Rose go and rest in the sun lounge while he cooked their dinner.

Puff and Ben curled up on the sofa next to Rose, which was a bit of a squash, but she didn't mind at all. There was something rather comforting about being snuggled up around warm, loving animals.

Rose was exhausted. It wasn't just the events of the past few days that had drained her but, indeed, the whole year had been crazy busy. A little voice inside her head kept saying, 'slow down.'

Tom and she hadn't had the time to even enjoy the summer, let alone to potter in the garden or sail on their boat.

Indeed, since returning from their European vacation last September, their feet had not touched the ground. In October they had driven out East to Nova Scotia to visit Anne in her new apartment in Halifax.

That had been a lovely visit and it was wonderful to see their daughter happy at last.

They had a quiet Christmas with just Jessica, Rob, Abby and Ella, then a slow couple of months, the calm before the storm.

April saw Paul and Atsuko's wedding in Japan followed by an amazing three-week travelling bonanza for Tom and Rose who were treated like royalty by all of Atsuko's relatives.

But it was all so exhausting and by the end of the three weeks they were longing to be back in the village where Spring had finally sprung and the garden had come alive, primarily with weeds, dandelions mostly.

It seemed that no sooner had they settled back home than preparations for the Canadian wedding to be held at the Town Hall had to be started.

Paul had said that it would be just a small affair but by the time he had finished making out the guest list there were just under one hundred people to be invited.

Rose had originally said that she would cater it herself and just serve canapés and cocktails as it was to be a sunset wedding service to be held in Pioneer Park and then back to the Town Hall for the reception.

That had been at the beginning of June. Since then, so much had happened. Rose felt quite dizzy thinking about it all. First, Tom had announced, out of the blue, that he was buying the car of his dreams.

This had totally surprised Rose who had no inkling that he was even looking at other cars. Their Volvo was only six years old and had served them well so that when he announced that he was getting an Audi Roadster TTS 2004 convertible, she was flabbergasted.

"What about Ben, where will he sit?" She had immediately asked when shown a picture of his dream car, which admittedly was very sleek and quite beautiful.

"Tom, don't you think that this is a little impractical?"

But Tom had just shrugged his shoulders and laughed. "Oh Rose, we're not getting rid of the Volvo, you can drive that. No, this is going to be my baby, my one and only indulgence."

Rose wasn't at all sure what to think of this change in her otherwise gentle, unassuming husband. Could it be a rather late male menopause that Tom was experiencing? She would have to keep a watchful eye for other symptoms.

She must have dozed off because Tom woke her with a gentle kiss. "Dinner is ready, love."

Puff and Ben jumped off the sofa and followed Rose to the table which was laid beautifully, and he had even lit a romantic candle. Tom had made a stir fry with shredded chicken, egg noodles, and loads of vegetables.

A lovely crisp, Iceberg lettuce with olives, sun ripe tomatoes, and salty feta cheese accompanied the dish. Rose absolutely adored a Greek salad.

"Thank you, Tom, my love. I really feel bushed. You know something, I was thinking about this past year. It's really been so very hectic, and I think that I'm beginning to feel my age."

"Yes, my love, but you don't look your age. Now hopefully we should have a quieter time now that summer is almost over. Have some wine, darling, and try to relax."

Just when dinner was almost eaten the telephone rang. Tom got up to answer it.

"Oh, hi, Anne. How are you my love?"

It was Anne, their daughter who had moved to Halifax. She was phoning to ask if she could come to visit.

"Dad, I would like you to meet Alan. He works with me at Dalhousie. We have some big news to tell you and Mom, but we'll wait until we come down next week."

Tom handed the phone over to Rose. Ten minutes later Rose put the phone down and came back to the table. "So much for a peaceful dinner. I wonder what's Anne's news? I bet that she's getting engaged. Oh, I wonder what Alan is like? Oh, Tom, I do hope that he's better than Seth."

Over the years, Anne had a series of misguided relationships ending last summer with Seth, who Rose and Tom were relieved to see depart from their daughter's life.

Anne and Alan were flying with Air Canada to Toronto and then on to London airport where Tom had agreed to meet them on

Tuesday evening. They were going to stay until the weekend and then go and visit Jessica and Rob and the girls in London.

Rose felt energized at the thought of seeing their daughter again after all this time.

Anne was their drama queen with a history of disastrous relationships. She hoped that this new one would prove the exception to the rule. *All parents ever want,* Rose thought, *is for their children to be happy,* and so far, happiness within a relationship seemed to have eluded their daughter Anne.

They would have to wait two long days before they found out Anne's big news. Rose couldn't wait. She telephoned Jessica. Sometimes she was left completely out of the loop with their daughters. On more than one occasion Jessica had known what was going on in either Anne or Paul's life way before Tom or herself. Sometimes Tom even knew before she was told.

"Oh, Jessica, this is mom here. I'm just phoning to let you know that Anne is flying in from Halifax on Tuesday. I think that she plans to visit you next weekend. She's bringing her new boyfriend, Alan. Do you know anything about him?"

"Oh mom, you're fishing, aren't you? Well, I don't know much other than the fact that Anne seems to be madly in love with him and that he is a fellow teacher at Dalhousie University. By the way, mom, Abby and Ella haven't stopped talking about Puff. He obviously made a big impression."

"Yes, well he's been rather mopey since the girls left. Anyway, my love, I had better go now. Give Abby and Ella a big hug. Love you."

Rose put the phone down and went to help clear away the dinner.

She was still speculating about Anne when they went to bed that night.

FIVE

Good morning everyone. Right. Let's have our reports. Who wants to go first? Sergeant Flowers, have you anything further to add about the black Mercedes?"

Sergeant Flowers stood up and opened his notebook.

"Yes, ma'am. Yesterday Rose Blair was followed from Goderich to Bayfield by the black Mercedes. She managed to get a very good description of him. It appears that he is short in stature, swarthy skinned, and has a black beard. She was so alarmed that she stopped off at the O.P.P. outside of Goderich and reported the stalking.

I looked into the registration again and the numbered company which no longer exists. I managed to trace down the original owners of this numbered company.

It was a dry-cleaning business in Montreal, but both owners are long gone since and the business is no longer. It might be worth checking with the Montreal police if there is any history connected to the business."

At the mention of Montreal, Susan immediately recalled her friend Henri Le Bruin. The previous September she had spent a few weekends up in Montreal with Henri but both of them had got tied up with work and it became more and more difficult to get time off to see each other. Their relationship just died before it had really got going. She might just give her old flame a call later on.

"Thank you, Sergeant Flowers. Right, anything else? Constable Mathieson, anymore on the crossbows?"

"Well, I checked with Canadian Tire and TSC in Goderich and they both sell crossbows which appear to retail at around $500. They also sell a number of different bolts for the crossbows. The sportswear shop in Kippen also sells crossbows and George Stokes has apparently bought a number of items of hunting gear from this shop."

"What about titanium arrows or bolts, as they're called?"

"All of the shops stock metal bolts however, only TSC sold a limited selection of titanium bolts and none of them matched the size of the bolt that killed Mary Stokes. That's all I've got to report, mam."

"Thank you, Constable Mathieson. Now, Constables Brown and Elliot, I gather that Sergeant Flowers asked if you could both look into the Croquet Club and bring back some background history and the membership list. Do you have one?"

"Yes, ma'am. We spoke to the President and he was more than willing to help us with the investigation. Apparently, the deceased only joined the club this year in May, actually the same time as Rose and Tom Blair.

Now the Croquet Club was founded in 1973 over forty years ago. It has been in its present location for only five years. Before that it was situated on a piece of land owned by Tom Cantrick, located on a farm called Foamy Acres, just five km. outside of Bayfield on Mill Street towards Varna."

Constable Brown cleared his throat and shuffled his papers before looking over to where Constable Elliot sat. He nodded his head in approval. Susan was about to tell the Constable to continue when he coughed again and picked up where he had left off.

"Women were only allowed to be members in 1993. It is actually an International Croquet Club and at one time was the only such inaugurated club in the whole of Canada. As to the membership, well, I interviewed quite a number of members and they all seemed a decent bunch. They hold cocktail parties every Thursday at 5:00 pm throughout the summer. Mary Stokes attended these parties along with her friend Rose. Everyone had good things to say about our victim apart from the Bradbury's, Alice and Dave, who lost their son, John, last year. He was involved with Jim Reynolds and the Montreal mobsters and was killed in a car accident during a police chase in Cambridge. Although Sergeant Flowers and Constable Mathieson had been on the team working the murder on Bayfield beach case the previous year, Constable Brown and Elliot were not familiar with the crime."

Brown continued with his report.

"Alice and Dave Bradbury had nothing to say about Mary Stokes but, by association, they railed on about Rose Blair for a good ten minutes accusing her of meddling in their lives and causing the death of their son, John. That's all I have to report, ma'am."

"Thank you, Constables Brown and Elliot. Interesting about the Bradbury's still hurting from last year. Anything else from the community at large?"

Constable Elliot opened up his notebook and proceeded to read from it, "Well, ma'am, once again it appears that Rose Blair has ruffled a few feathers and dragged our victim, Mary Stokes, into the snare. Apparently, there was some issue over the Historical Society's new Heritage Centre. It appears that Rose Blair was quite opinionated about some of the planning and brought Mary Stokes into the debate. Several people mentioned that both women were quite upset by the whole affair. That's all I have to report."

"Thank you everyone. Constable Mathieson and I have made some progress. It looks as if we might have a prime suspect, George Stokes. He is currently unemployed, with a record of multiple visits to the Blue Water Detention Centre, a habitual drug user, but more importantly, he is a crossbow hunter. So, we have the means and the opportunity, yet the motive is unclear. Constable Elliot, has anything come back yet from our computer lab?"

"Well, ma'am, I got a printout of all the emails sent and received on Mary Stokes' computer. There were the usual online banking payments, not a lot of correspondence, no Facebook account or Twitter, in fact her social media was restricted to just emails.

There was one contact, however, of interest. I've highlighted it in yellow. Pierre La Ville. I ran his name through our computer banks and for some reason his name came back as guarded, blocked. I'm looking into this further, ma'am, and hope to have some information by tomorrow."

"Thank you, Constable. Right, Constable Mathieson and I hope to interview George Stokes later on today. The rest of you, keep digging. I feel that we are getting closer to the truth. So, same time tomorrow."

Susan watched her team disperse and then she got out her cell phone and called her friend, Inspector Henri Le Bruin in Montreal.

"Ma cherie, Susie, comment ca va?"

"Oh Henri, please speak English," Susan said with a smile. She knew perfectly well that Henri could speak just perfect English although there was something so erotic about listening to a French man speak. Hearing Henri again stirred up all sorts of sensual feelings. Since her last fling with online dating several months ago, Susan had not had a decent or satisfactory date. It was lonely being a single career woman at the top of the game.

"So, my little butterfly, how can this humble French man be of service?"

"Henri, I have a couple of favours to ask of you. We are trying to track down a black Mercedes registered to a numbered company in Quebec. Could you see if you can find out more about this vehicle and the ownership? Secondly, I have a name of a French man, Pierre La Ville. We found it on the computer of our murder victim.

Normally we would be able to trace all names in our large

computer database, but this name seems to have been tagged. It is important to us to know why it is blocked. I just thought that as he obviously was French maybe you might have more luck tracking him down in Quebec than we have here in Ontario."

Susan could hear Henri tapping away on his computer. A few minutes later he said.

"Ah, *voila*. I can help you with the black Mercedes. The dry-cleaning business was originally owned by a Serbian couple, Mikail and Teresa Bratanek. Mikail Bratanek had a business partner called Riva Strugar. This partner had connections to a Serbian syndicate quite active in the 90's.

We thought that it had died out, but recently we have seen a resurgence of gang warfare with the Serbs at the front lines. As to this Pierre La Ville, well, if his name has been blocked that probably means he is a government agent. Could be Inland Revenue, Customs, Immigration, or anything Federal. If you leave it with me, I'll find out. Now, ma cherie, when are you and I going to get together again?"

Susan had no sooner put the telephone down when it rang again. She answered it quickly.

"Oh, hi Susan, it's Rose. Tom and I were wondering if you would like to come around for dinner tonight. We've got our daughter Anne and her boyfriend arriving tomorrow so the rest of the week will be taken up with their visit, but we'd love to have you join us if you can around 7:00pm?"

"Oh, thank you. Yes, I'd love to come. I'll bring a bottle of wine. See you then."

With her phone put away Susan collected up her papers and prepared to leave the Lion's Hall. Her mind was preoccupied with two things Henri had said. Firstly, he had mentioned that Europol had contacted Interpol.

Jim Reynolds had managed to evade detection for one year but had just been identified by a passport scanned into the system when he was travelling as a Dutch businessman under the name of Gert

Boursima. He was seen entering Turkey, but unfortunately, by the time the police had matched up his face with that of one Jim Reynolds, he was long gone into the crowded city of Istanbul.

The Turkish police had been notified. They were closing in on him and Susan felt uncomfortable with her feelings. On the one hand she wanted him to be caught and sentenced but, on the other hand, she couldn't help but remember the good times that they had shared together.

The second thing that had given Susan pause for thought was the fact that Henri had a conference in London and was going to come to Bayfield to visit her.

I must get my hair done, had been Susan's immediate thought as she locked up the Lions Hall and walked to her car. She looked across to the Spa, *I might also have a bikini wax and pedicure too,* she mused as a thrill of excitement ran down her spine. Henri had that effect on her. Every nerve in her body came alive at the thought of him running his hands over her body.

ROSE GEARED INTO ACTION. She loved cooking, particularly for dinner parties. Maybe she would invite Doug to make up a foursome. Doug had been widowed for a few years now and, although he appeared happy enough, Rose thought that he must get very lonely on his own.

She picked up the phone and called him and sure enough he was thrilled at the prospect of dinner.

Doug answered the phone with his deep baritone voice.

"But Rose, no matchmaking. I'm past all of that and honestly, I've got used to my own company. Mind you, I will never turn down a good meal. I get a bit tired of microwave dinners."

With that settled Rose got down to cooking. She would make Tom's favourite – steak and Guinness pie and serve it with roast potatoes, cauliflower au gratin, carrots, and green beans.

She thought about the starter and dessert while opening the fridge and peering inside. There was a load of tomatoes from the garden, mushrooms, and an assortment of cheeses, cream, salad stuff, and strawberries.

Rose decided to make a chilled gazpacho soup and serve that with artisan bread crostini. For dessert she would make crème de chocolate with stuffed strawberries.

Tom had disappeared off after lunch to work on the boat, leaving Rose to her cooking. Ben and Puff flopped down on the cool kitchen floor strategically placed to catch any tidbits of food that might fall their way. Rose made the soup first as it had to chill in the fridge for at least four hours before serving.

She next made up the artisan bread dough and putting it in a bowl inside a plastic bag, she placed it outside in the sun on the patio table to rise. Rose then washed and hulled the strawberries and cut off the pointy bottoms so that they would stand upright, she then scooped out the flesh forming little strawberry cups big enough to stuff with the sweetened cream cheese.

They looked delicious as Rose placed them in the fridge to chill. Lastly, she made the steak and Guinness pie using the last can of Tom's Guinness.

It was five o'clock by the time she had finished preparing the meal. Next, Rose decided to take a quick shower and then a change into a summer dress. She was in the shower when Tom came home.

"Oh, darling, can you put some wine in the fridge and set the table. You know that Susan is coming for dinner and I've also invited Doug."

Tom had come into the bathroom looking sun tanned and handsome in his white shorts and turquoise Polo t-shirt which really brought out the blue of his eyes. Rose's heart fluttered and she felt like a twenty-year-old again. Standing there with a towel wrapped around her and with her hair dripping wet, she pulled Tom to her saying, "Have I told you lately that I love you?"

The dinner party could wait...

AFTER THE PHONE call from Rose, Susan jumped in her car and drove up to the Subway shop on the highway. She was starving but didn't have time to have lunch at one of the restaurants in town.

She ordered a foot-long sub filled with cold cuts, tomatoes, lettuce, onions, pickles, and mayonnaise. The girl cut the sub in half and wrapped each half up separately. Susan would give one half to Constable Mathieson, and they could eat on their way to Kippen where they were going to interview George Stokes.

Twenty minutes later they pulled up outside the dreary bungalow. Jean Stokes was outside taking down her laundry from a washing line strung up between two trees. She nodded a greeting to them and told them to go inside where George was waiting. Susan and Constable Mathieson entered the house.

George Stokes was sitting at the dining room table playing a game of Patience with a well-worn deck of cards. He looked up as they came in and gruffly said, "I've done nothing wrong, you know."

Susan was surprised by George's voice and manner.

Constantly in her line of work she had to remind herself not to pre-judge or to have any presuppositions about people.

It was so easy to be judgmental and to put people into stereotypes. In this case, unwittingly, Susan had imagined George to be the typical drug user.

Instead, in front of her sat a handsome young man, well groomed, nicely spoken and seemingly polite. She put out her hand and said," George, I presume. I am Inspector Parker, and this is Constable Mathieson. We just have a few questions to ask you about Mary Stokes. It will only take a few minutes of your time."

George turned to Susan and shook her hand. She was able to look at him more closely. He was certainly a good-looking man and she could definitely see the resemblance to his father, Graham, although there was something about his eyes that made her feel uncomfortable.

"It came as a shock when mom told me about her death. Murder wasn't it?"

"Yes, we're trying to find out as much about her as we can, and we know that you still kept in touch. When was the last time that you saw her?"

George looked away and pondered.

"You know something, I can't quite remember. Maybe at the beginning of the summer?"

"Do you come to Bayfield at all?"

"Yes. My mates and I like to visit every now and then. The Albion is our watering hole of choice."

"When were you last at the Albion?"

"I can't remember."

Susan started to get irritated by his vague answers. She thought that he was being deliberately obtuse as she signalled with her eyes to Constable Mathieson to take the lead.

Constable Mathieson cleared his throat and spoke. "George, we understand that you own a crossbow?"

George looked surprised by the change of tack.

"Yes, I go hunting and the crossbow is the best. It's silent and more accurate than a rifle."

"What bolts do you use?"

"Now you're talking my talk. Mostly I use ten-inch carbon fibre tipped bolts, but if I'm going deer hunting, I use Titanium 12-inch bolts. Mind you, they're expensive so I limit their use. Why all the hunting questions?"

"Umm... well... Mary Stokes was killed by a crossbow."

"You're looking at me as a possible murderer? Do you know how many people in Huron County own crossbows? Let me tell you, hundreds."

George had stood up and immediately Susan felt threatened by the six-foot something man fuming in front of them.

'We're not accusing you of anything, but the truth of the matter is you knew Mary Stokes and you own a crossbow. We deal with facts, George, and those are two undeniable facts. Now, maybe you could tell us where you were on August 4th at 8.45 a.m.?"

George sat down again and put his head in his hands.

"Okay, I'll admit to being in Bayfield on the previous evening, that was August 3rd. I was with my friends at the Albion. I spent the night with my mate, Tyler, and ended up sleeping at his place until about mid- day. I'd had one too many the night before. Tyler drove me home and I got here at about 1:30 p.m."

Constable Mathieson wrote everything down in his notebook.

"I presume that we'll be able to verify all of this? Can we have your friends address and contact numbers? I'm sure that Kim at The Albion will know you if you're a regular. What can you tell us about Mary Stokes?"

George seemed to visibly relax. He let out a big sigh and answered the question with a monotone voice.

"When I was fourteen my mom and dad split up. Dad hit the bottle too much and mom couldn't take it anymore. He remarried a couple of years later and his new wife, Mary was like a breath of fresh air. To begin with, dad stopped drinking, and everything was cool.

I used to visit them every other weekend. Mom would drive me to Guelph, and I'd spend a couple of days with Dad and Mary. She was always kind to me although I wasn't exactly easy to be around.

She used to say that she was lucky to have a son to love. She made me feel wanted and special. Of course, I screwed it all up with the drugs, but even then, when I was detained at the Blue Water Youth Correctional Centre, she would send me care packages with little notes of encouragement."

"Did she ever talk to you about her life before your dad or about her family?"

"No, not really, although I did get the impression that they were all dead. The other thing that I found odd was that in the early days when I first met her, she used to speak with a slight foreign accent. I thought that she was maybe from Quebec, you know, French or something but when I asked her, she flatly denied that she was French."

"Is there anything else that you can tell us about Mary?"

George thought for a minute.

"No, not really except for the fact that I always thought that she was hiding something. Then dad hit the bottle again and mom stopped dropping me off and I stopped visiting him. Mary and dad split up. I was quite sad when they did, but Mary wrote to me and told me that I was still like a son to her no matter what. She used to send me $20 every now and then. I feel really bad that I never thanked her for the money, ever."

"Well, George, thank you very much. You've been most helpful. Here's my card, if there's anything else that you can think of don't hesitate to contact me."

Susan handed over a business card and got ready to leave. She waved to Jean Stokes who was still in the back yard folding laundry.

Constable Mathieson and Susan drove back to Bayfield both deep in thought.

DOUG ARRIVED FIRST CARRYING a half pack of Boddington's beer and a lovely bunch of flowers for Rose.

Tom offered him a drink and they had just settled down in the sunroom when Susan arrived. She looked stunning in an off the shoulder blue silk sheath with a glittery lace shawl draped over her tanned shoulders.

She wore blue high heel shoes that made her legs look like a model. Her hair was gleaming, and her face made up beautifully. Rose felt immediately under dressed and frumpy in her sun dress.

Even though she had made a bit of an effort to dress up no way could she ever compete with the sophistication of Susan Parker.

If it wasn't for the fact that they were old friends, she could easily have been quite jealous.

The dinner went well and then the conversation turned to the murder enquiry. Doug wanted to know how the investigation was progressing. Susan replied cautiously.

"You know something, Doug, the public have it in their heads that the police need to solve a murder within a few days. I think that television has propagated this myth. Many murder cases take weeks and even months to solve.

There are an awful lot of questions to be answered and much leg work. It is true that 75% of murders are committed by a close relative but not always. In Mary Stokes' case she had very few close relatives and I can assure you that we are looking at those quite thoroughly."

Rose asked Susan about the black Mercedes and whether there was any connection to the murder case.

"We have some interesting information that connects the vehicle to a Serbian syndicate based out of Montreal. How this is connected to you, or indeed, to the Mary Stokes murder, we have yet to discover. I can assure you that we will leave no stone unturned in this inquiry."

Later, while they were clearing away, Rose asked Susan about Jim Reynolds.

"I have to tell you something, Susan. Tom and I felt really bad that we didn't report our sighting of him in the café in Vienna. I suppose if we had he might have been caught by now?"

"Oh Rose, don't beat yourself up over that after all this time. Tom did, after all, email me and I contacted Interpol straight away. If you must know, Jim has been spotted entering Turkey. He is somewhere in Istanbul right now. We're closing in on him."

The evening wrapped up, Doug and Susan departed, and Rose and Tom decided to leave the clearing away until the following morning. They were both dog tired. Anne and Alan were arriving the next day and they had much to do before their arrival.

SIX

Susan got up early and decided to go for a swim before meeting up with her team. She did her best thinking when doing laps in a pool and she certainly had much to think about.

The team was all gathered in The Lion's Hall when Susan arrived.

"Good morning everyone. Let's have all the reports. Constables Brown and Elliot, anything more to report from the local people of Bayfield?"

Constable Brown stood up and prepared to speak.

"Ma'am, we seem to have exhausted finding anything about Mary from the people of Bayfield. We did, however, make some enquiries in Goderich and Clinton. At Elliot's Liquidation in Clinton the owner remembered Mary.

He said that he got the distinct impression that she was on hard times.

He said that he could always recognize the people who were just after a bargain from those who truly had little money to spare.

He rarely saw her with anyone, and she always came in on a

Saturday at the same time, at 10:30 a.m. In Goderich it appears that she often shopped at the Salvation Army charity shop on Sun Coast Drive.

The shop keeper recognized the photograph I was showing around. The charity shop said that she bought a lot of her clothes there and always paid cash.

She also said that she could have sworn that Mary was from Germany or somewhere in Europe. She reckoned that she could hear it in her accent. I thought, with your permission, ma'am, I would run her name through our Interpol data base and see if anything comes up."

"Thank you, Constable. Yes, go ahead and run her name through the system. Anything else from the community?"

"No, ma'am, although something did occur to me. Mary Stokes was murdered in the Bayfield Cemetery. Maybe we should be asking the grounds keeper there if he heard or saw anything out of the ordinary.

I took the liberty of checking out his name. He is one Mike Powell of Goshen Line. If you don't mind, ma'am, I will go ahead and contact him after this meeting."

"Yes, great, good thinking. Constable Mathieson, anything more on the black Mercedes?"

"Well, ma'am, there have been no further sightings. I did contact the Montreal police and they have nothing further to add on the extinct numbered company. Sorry, we seem to have reached a dead end with the mystery Mercedes."

Susan fidgeted with her notebook.

"I spoke to Inspector Henri Le Bruin in Montreal. He told me that the dry-cleaning business which the car was registered under had connections with a Serbian syndicate which was pretty active in the 90's.

Then all activity on that front seemed to go quiet for a number of years so much so that the police thought that the syndicate had been disbanded. Recently, though, Serbian gangs have been fighting again.

Now, what any of this might have to do with our black Mercedes, who can tell, but Inspector Le Bruin is very kindly looking into it for us."

Susan glanced over to where Constable Mathieson was sitting and gave him an encouraging smile before continuing.

"Now, Constable Mathieson and I interviewed George Stokes. He not only possesses a crossbow, but he also uses titanium bolts similar to the one that killed Mary Stokes. He was also in Bayfield at the time of the murder. His alibi does, however, stand up. He was at The Albion the night before the murder and had drank a lot of beers. We have no actual proof that he slept until mid-day other than what his friend, Tyler, told us which verifies his story. George had no transport of his own and his friend Tyler's place is way over in Jowett's Grove which is rather a long walk to the Croquet Club for anyone let alone someone suffering from a hangover. We have not ruled George Stokes out completely. There is something not quite transparent about him. I feel that he isn't being completely honest with us. Now, Sergeant Flowers, I want a complete bio on our Mary Stokes. Place of birth, parents, siblings, which schools and college she attended, where she lived before she met Graham Stokes. So far, we have nothing about her early life. Keep digging, men. We are getting closer to the truth. Same time tomorrow. Constable Mathieson, may I have a word with you before you depart?"

The rest of the team disbanded leaving the Constable in the room with Susan.

"How can I help you, ma'am?"

"Constable, I want you to go back to Hensall and look at George's hunting gear. Ask around Exeter and Kippen. I just feel intuitively that George is hiding something from us. Take Sergeant Flowers with you."

Susan dismissed the constable and sat down at her computer

preparing to write up a report to Headquarters. The Chief would be expecting results and somehow what she had to report was painfully scant.

TOM WAS DETERMINED to pick Anne and Alan up in his new car. Rose told him that they would never all fit in the convertible as there was barely a back seat. Tom had just laughed and said that only Anne was small, and she could easily squeeze into the space behind the driver's seat.

When Rose thought of Tom with his new 'toy,' she always conjured up an image of Toad in 'Toad of Toad Hall' driving in his sports car creating havoc wherever he went. Tom was not a reckless driver, in fact, he was a really good driver, but this new acquisition gave Rose pause for thought.

Whilst she loved her husband dearly, she was aware that his behaviour had been a little strange and out of character these past few months. A delayed male menopause maybe, but whatever it was it had Rose somewhat perplexed.

Tom and she had spent the morning cleaning the house, putting fresh sheets and towels in the guest bedroom and, as usual, Rose set to baking.

She decided to make some puff pastry tartlets stuffed with cream cheese and stilton with a slice of pear on top. They would make good hors' d'oeuvres.

Tom had suggested that they have a bar-b-que. Rose bought some salmon fillets and some giant prawns which she threaded onto kebab skewers and left to marinade in a lemon and ginger sauce.

Making a potato, celery, apple, and walnut salad, she tossed together a medley of green leaves from the garden and quickly made her favourite maple syrup dressing. The artisan bread was already to be cooked, the patio table set, all Rose had to do was brush her hair and freshen up her lipstick.

She expected Tom back with Anne and Alan any minute.

Their plane arrived bang on time at London Airport. Tom pulled up to the car park at the same time as the passengers were alighting from the plane. Tom saw Anne before she saw him.

She looked positively glowing, Tom thought and then his eyes drifted to the man standing next to her with his hand casually draped around her shoulder in a proprietary manner.

He looked at least ten years older than his daughter, in fact, he looked almost as old as Tom, which quite shocked him. Alan was about 5 feet 11 inches with an angular body, a sharp nose, and rimless glasses.

He had light brown hair with a receding forehead, a generous mouth, and quite narrow set eyes. Anne started to wave, and Tom smiled and waved back. Soon they were standing in the car park admiring Tom's Audi Roadster TTS. Alan seemed to know his cars.

"Is it a 3.2 litre engine, Tom?" He asked having peered intently at the silver beast before them.

"Yes, it's got six cylinders, 250 horsepower and it purrs like a kitten. The only problem is there isn't really a proper back seat. Anne, my love, I'm afraid you're going to have to sit sideways. Fortunately, we haven't got far to go."

"Oh, Dad, I don't mind. She's a beauty. I love the fact that it's a convertible. What does Mom think?"

Tom laughed, "Your mom thinks that I've gone off my rocker, but she's let me indulge myself with this simple pleasure."

They squeezed their luggage into the small trunk and Anne climbed into the back while Alan and Tom stretched their legs out in front. The engine growled to life and Tom expertly steered the Audi out of the car park and on to the highway.

Ben announced their arrival with a series of loud, excited barks. Puff joined in although he hadn't a clue why Ben was barking.

Anne burst into the house and hugged Rose.

"Mom, it's so great to be home. Wow, that Audi Roadster is quite the car. I feel as if I've been thrown in the tumble drier. Just look at my hair, it's like a bird's nest, all tangled up!"

Alan came through the front door followed by Tom carrying two suitcases. Ben danced around Anne's legs and Puff sniffed her feet.

"Oh, Mom, who is this funny looking dog?"

Rose put her arms around Puff's neck. "This is Puff. He's come to live with us. He used to belong to my friend Mary, but we've adopted him now."

"What sort of breed is he? He looks a bit like a small golden retriever although he has pointy ears. Funny face, aren't you Puffy? He's actually quite adorable, mom, I love him already."

"Well, you and Abby and Ella too! I think that Puff has settled in very easily. I'll tell you his story later but right now I want to meet Alan."

"Sorry, Mom and Dad, can I introduce to you Alan?"

Alan put out his hand to shake. Rose ignored it and instead gave him a big hug.

"So lovely to meet you, Alan. Let me show you to your room and then you can come outside to join us for a drink. Tom's heating up the bar-b-que. I hope that you eat salmon?"

Rose left Anne and Alan to freshen up while she put out the hors d'oeuvres.

She wasn't sure what to think of Alan. He certainly seemed much older than she had expected, but he seemed kind and Anne did look exuberantly happy.

Dinner went well. Alan was easy going and a natural conversationalist. He appeared comfortable in his own skin.

Anne seemed so happy, but Rose was just afraid that her bubble would burst as she couldn't fathom out why her daughter could be having a relationship with a man so much older than herself. She was determined to find out who Alan really was.

"Alan, you work at Dalhousie? Have you been there long?"

"Yes, almost fifteen years. I was at McGill before. I can actually retire anytime but I love my subject and enjoy teaching."

"Anne told me that you are an astrophysicist. Forgive my ignorance, but what exactly do you do? Something to do with astrology I presume?"

Alan laughed his easy going laugh. "I work primarily with calculations. Quantum physics, calculating distances between stars and planets. There is a fabulous observatory in Halifax."

"They've just opened one in London. Tom, isn't there also someone off Highway 21 close to Goderich who has an observatory?

I used to think that it was a farm silo with a dome on top, but someone told me that the dome retracted and there was a powerful telescope inside. Quite amazing."

Alan was thoughtful for a moment.

"It's not often that individuals own their own observatory. It's actually one of my dreams to build my own. I wouldn't mind meeting the owners while I'm down here if that would be at all possible?"

Tom nodded and said that he would make some enquiries.

"Now, Alan, do you own your own house in Halifax?" Rose knew that she was shamelessly fishing for information, but she ploughed away all the same.

"Yes, actually I've got an apartment just down the road from the university and a cottage in Marguerite in Cape Breton."

Anne knew exactly what her mother was doing. She decided to intervene.

"Mom, I'm sure that Alan won't mind me telling you that he has an ex-wife and two children, well, hardly children. Dave and Missy are both at university."

Rose looked a bit embarrassed, but at least the air was cleared, and she could stop her fishing. Anne laughed and squeezed her mother's hand. "Mom, loosen up, more people divorce than stay together these days.

Just because you and dad have been together for 43 years it just proves that you both are the exception to the rule."

Rose and Tom looked at each other and nodded. What most people didn't realize was that all marriages had their ups and downs and theirs was no exception. One had to work at any relationship and Rose suspected that young couples were not prepared to put enough energy or effort into keeping their marriages viable.

But just what was she to think about a man old enough to be their daughter's father, married once before with two grown up children? *I'll have to be more liberal minded*, Rose thought as Tom prepared to speak.

"So, Anne, Alan, what is the big news. You've had your mother and I on tenterhooks trying to guess what it is you have to tell us."

Alan took Anne's hand and they both smiled. Anne took the lead.

"Mom, Dad, I'm expecting a baby. Alan and I are having a baby together."

Rose looked shocked. She had honestly expected that they were going to announce an engagement or that they had moved in with each other, but not a baby. Although, it had crossed her mind briefly when Anne declined any wine and opted for tonic water instead. But a baby with Alan?

She recovered herself suitably enough to say.

'Wow, that's amazing news, darling. When is the baby due?"

Anne did not look at all pregnant. She was positively blooming and radiant with good health. Who would have guessed that she was actually expecting a baby!

"I'm just three months. The baby is due in February. Oh, Mom, Dad, we're so excited. I haven't felt at all sick. No morning sickness. I've just gone off drinking coffee and I don't like the smell of fried food but that's all!"

Rose looked at her daughter and couldn't help but smile. Anne had charged through life like an effervescent firework. She sparkled and glittered and lit up the whole room with her positive joie de vivre. How could anyone resist such enthusiasm? She only prayed that Alan would keep the sparkle alive and well.

"We should make a toast to you both." Tom said as he topped up Alan and Rose's wine glasses and poured some more tonic water into Anne's glass.

"To Alan and Anne and the baby." They all chinked their glasses together.

Later Rose called Anne into the kitchen to help serve the dessert. "I've made your favourite whiskey ice cream, my love, but I guess a little alcohol won't do you any harm."

Rose often made this quick dessert when rushed from blending ice cream with a glass of whiskey and then spooning the mixture into wine glasses, sprinkling grated chocolate on top and placing a sponge finger into the mixture.

It was Jessica and Anne's favourite dessert and one of the easiest one's that Rose knew how to make.

The rest of the evening went by smoothly. Anne and Alan retired to bed early and Rose and Tom, after clearing away the plates and loading up the dishwasher put Ben and Puff into the garden and prepared themselves for an early night.

SEVEN

Susan had a quiet evening the night before, in fact, after a quick lasagne dinner at DaVinci's, she had gone back to The Bayfield Village Inn, swam fifty lengths of the pool, and then went to bed. She had watched television for an hour and then turned out her light at 9:00 p.m.

This morning she had awoken feeling quite relaxed and ready to face the day with renewed energy.

The team was gathered, the coffee on, an air of anticipation filled the air.

"Good morning everyone. Let's have your reports. Constable Brown, how did it work out with Michael Powell, the cemetery grounds man?"

Constable Brown stood up to speak.

"I had a long talk with the man yesterday and you will all find what he had to say very interesting. Michael lives in a small trailer parked behind a farmhouse about 5 kilometres down the Goshen Line. He was quite friendly and easy to talk to. Currently he is employed by the Blue Water Municipality to cut the grass and generally keep the cemetery in good order. When he was asked if he knew the deceased, he nodded his head and seemed visibly distraught. You see, it appears that Mary Stokes and Michael Powell have been having a relationship this past six months. They had been very discreet as he didn't want his ex-wife finding out as they apparently are right in the middle of a legal battle, and he didn't want to add fuel to the fire. He met Mary when he noticed her visiting the graves on a regular basis. She would come to the cemetery once or twice a week bringing flowers and arranging them on neglected children's graves. He observed her doing this for weeks before they spoke to each other."

Constable Brown paused while he read through his notes before continuing.

"When he asked her why she was tending the graves she said that she missed her own children more than anything else in the world. By honouring other children's graves, it felt like she was tending to her own children. He said that it sounded weird, but one had to have been there to hear her explanation. It made sense when she explained it to him. He liked her very much. When she had finished fussing over the graves she would go and sit on one of the benches and he would sometimes join her and they would talk. They fell naturally into a physical relationship with a kiss at first and then he invited her back to his place and one thing led to another. They were having this relationship right up to the day before she died."

Susan interrupted Constable Brown by saying, "Did you ask him where he was on the morning of August 4th?"

"Yes, ma'am. Apparently, he worked at the cemetery three days a week and August 4th was not one of them. He found out about Mary's death when he was at The Albion. They were all discussing the murder and he said that it came as a huge shock to him."

"Thank you, Constable. I might drive over and have a little talk with Mr. Powell myself. Sergeant Flowers and Constable Mathieson, how did you get on with questioning people in the Exeter area?"

Constable Mathieson opened up his notebook. "I went back to

the Kippen Sportswear Shop and asked the owner a few questions. George Stokes was a regular customer. He has never had any problems with George although his friend Tyler, is another matter. In fact, Tyler is on my list of people I want to interview. I spoke to Sergeant Burrell's of the Exeter O.P.P. detachment. He had known George since he was a teenager. He said that George basically was a good kid who had been led astray by peer pressure."

Constable Mathieson referred back to his notes before continuing.

"At one stage he was into Crystal Meth or 'glass,' as they like to call it locally. George was also involved in an illegal lab found using chemically altered over the counter drugs like allergy medicine or cold remedies.

As far as Sergeant Burrell's was aware George was now clean of drugs and going straight. I met with Tyler Walker, George's friend and it is true, he does keep his hunting gear in Tyler's shed.

I photographed George's crossbow and bolts, but they all look alike, just like the ones that I saw in Canadian Tire and TSC.

I haven't yet found anything to implicate George for the murder of Mary Stokes."

"Thank you, Constable. Sergeant Flowers, any joy with Mary Stokes' bio?"

"I entered her name into the federal computer database and cross-referenced it with her social insurance number and her driver's licence. All that came back was what we already know. Mary married Graham and worked as a secretary at St. Vincent's School in Guelph. I did, however, ascertain her maiden name. It was Mary Watson and her address before being married was 9 Carlisle Place, Guelph. I checked this out and found it to be an apartment block on the south side of the city within walking distance of the school. Nobody could remember her living there but it was fifteen years ago. It does seem strange that I can find no record pre-dating 1996."

Susan thought for a minute and then said, "What about her driver's license. When was that first issued?"

"According to the license data base Mary Watson was issued her first driver's license on July 22nd, 1996. I am sorry, ma'am. That appears to be all I can find out about Mary Stokes, or should I say, Mary Watson.

I could find no record of her birth certificate or any records pertaining to her parents or siblings, if she had any."

"Thank you, Constable. I think that we need to get Mary Stokes name into the international database. It could be that she was born overseas and only came to Canada in 1996. Good work, Sergeant Flowers.

Now, anymore reports on the black Mercedes?"

Constable Elliot stood up and referred to his notes.

"Yesterday at 5:45 p.m. a security camera on the roof of the Shell garage in Seaforth, picked up this photo of a black Mercedes filling up with gas. Look, the bearded man is standing next to the gas nozzle. See the license plate. That's our guy."

Susan looked at the photograph taken from the security camera. It was pretty grainy but there was no doubt that she was looking at the black Mercedes which had been stalking Rose and Tom Blair.

The big question is, was the Mercedes leaving the area or was Seaforth its base?

"Constable, dispatch an O.P.P. car immediately to Seaforth and keep a surveillance on the town. If the Mercedes is there we need to know and quickly.

Right, the rest of you, keep digging. We will unearth the truth bit by bit. See you all tomorrow, same time."

Susan packed up her computer and looked at her watch. She had made an appointment to have a bikini wax and a pedicure at The Spa for 2:00 p.m. It was now 1:00 p.m., time enough for lunch. Rose had told Susan about The Sunset Diner's sushi bar.

She loved sushi, not the raw fish variety but the Californian sushi with avocado, cucumber, and carrots. It had to be freshly made and the quality of the sushi that Susan had eaten varied tremendously.

This would be a good way to see if The Sunset Diner would pass her test.

Susan drove up the highway to the south side of the village. It really quite amazed her that the tiny village of Bayfield should have such a variety of restaurants. To have both a sushi and a Thai restaurant, plus the other good eateries along the main street in a village with a population of barely 800, was nothing short of remarkable.

THIRTY MINUTES later Susan was eating some of the best Sushi that she had ever eaten. The owners of the restaurant were Korean, but they had a passion for Sushi.

The food was beautifully presented on red and black lacquered platters with tiny dishes of pickled ginger and Wasabi paste. Lovely pottery tea pots of ginseng tea were served with every meal.

Susan left feeling very satisfied and happy. She would certainly recommend the sushi to everyone. Next time she would bring Henri Le Bruin to eat at The Sunset Diner.

ANNE AND ALAN slept in late. By the time that they finally appeared for breakfast, Rose had made a batch of pineapple and raisin scones and a mushroom and cheese frittata for their breakfast.

Tom had gone off for a game of golf with Doug, but he had given Rose strict instructions to let Anne and Alan know that he would take them out for a sail in the afternoon, weather permitting.

Over breakfast, Rose told Anne and Alan about the murder at the Croquet Club. She decided to keep the threatening Mercedes to herself. There was no need to worry her daughter needlessly.

"So, mom, are you going to do some of your sleuthing like last year? I thought it was pretty cool what you did with photographing those silver pieces and looking it up online."

Rose looked pensive. "I wish that I could be of some help to the police because it doesn't sound as if they're making much headway with the investigation. My friend was lovely, but she was so very private. They can't seem to trace any of her family. It's as if she never existed before getting married in 1998."

"Well, mom, maybe she never existed in Canada, but she must have existed somewhere. My guess is that she immigrated from across the Atlantic and left all her family behind."

Rose thought for a while.

"But why didn't she tell me? We were quite close friends, and I really knew nothing about her."

"Oh Mom, she probably didn't tell you because she wanted to forget her old life. If you move to another country you can start a fresh life, a new leaf and create a person with no connections to the past."

Rose was thoughtful. "You know something, Anne, you've become such a wise, old lady."

"Hey, mom, less of the old, but seriously, how can you help the murder enquiry? You're good at asking questions, look at you last night with Alan!"

"Yes, my love, but the police have been interviewing everyone in the community. The trouble is Mary didn't belong to many things. Our fitness class was the only community class that she liked."

"Well, she must have done something other than go to fitness classes!" Anne said with exasperation.

Rose thought and then said, "Actually, several times a week she would visit the cemetery. I thought that it was odd. Once, I asked if I could go with her. It was weird. She spent an hour tidying up the graves of children. She even bought flowers to put on their graves."

"Did you ever ask her why she was doing that, Mom?"

"Yes, of course I did, and she just said that children should never be neglected both in life and in death."

"Oh, mom, that sounds so creepy."

"But it wasn't. Mary was quite happy pottering around the cemetery; she even hummed to herself as she worked. Come to think of it there was a man, a work man, tending to the graves and I got the impression that they knew each other quite well."

Anne shrieked. "Well, mom, there you are, you've got your first person to interview. I bet that he knew her very well if she was going so frequently to the cemetery. That's where you should first start. I tell you what, why don't we both pop over there now? Alan wants to read the newspaper, but I really could do with some fresh air. How about a lovely walk around the cemetery on this beautiful, sunny morning?"

Rose smiled at her daughters' enthusiasm. It wouldn't do any harm, she thought as she poured out more coffee, in fact she had been meaning to go back to the cemetery to have a serious look at the head stones.

"Yes, well it will make a nice change to walk through the cemetery. By the way, while you're here you should take Alan on some of the trail walks. They're all lovely, although my favourite is the Sawmill Creek Trail down by the Bayfield River."

With their morning planned Rose set to tidying up the kitchen. She let the dogs out into the garden and then sat at the table with a note pad in her hands.

What will I cook for dinner tonight, Rose thought while writing out a shopping list.

In the end she decided on making a Moussaka as there was an egg plant in the fridge that needed using and she always had ground mince in the freezer. She would make a lemon meringue pie for dessert as she had plenty of lemons, oh, and a large Greek salad.

There was still some artisan bread dough left in the fridge which she would shape up and bake fresh for the evening. Rose had already decided to take Alan and Anne out for lunch, but hadn't yet decided where. She would leave that choice up to them.

Anne appeared having changed into a pair of shorts and a t-shirt. *She looks like a teenager*, Rose thought as they prepared to leave. Who would have ever guessed that she was pregnant?

"Are you sure that you're alright being left on your own, Alan?" Rose said as she let the dogs back in.

Alan, who had made himself comfortable in the sunroom smiled and said, "Well, I'm hardly on my own with the dogs keeping me company, but no, I enjoy reading The Globe and Mail. When I've finished, I might just take these two for a walk."

"Well, I'll leave you a front door key and their leashes are hanging up in the hall. See you later."

Rose and Anne left driving off in the Volvo headed for the cemetery.

When they arrived at the entrance Anne exclaimed.

"Mom, it's so pretty, the trees form almost an archway. I must take a photograph of this. I could use this in one of my film shorts."

They drove down the graveled entranceway and parked the car at the top. It was totally peaceful, the way a graveyard should be in respect of the dead. Rose looked over towards the fence that separated the cemetery from the Croquet Club.

Was it only a week since she had found her dear friend, Mary, slumped over the headstone? She could see the remains of the yellow tape where the police had cordoned off the crime scene. Anne followed her mother's gaze.

"Is that where it happened, Mom?"

Rose replied with a shaky voice, "Yes, dear, it was dreadful. I'll never forget the nightmarish scene. It's been etched into my head forever. Poor, poor Mary."

They were both distracted by voices from the Croquet Club. Rose recognized a few. Tom and she had hadn't played Croquet since the murder and they had missed the last cocktail party. They probably would miss the upcoming one too.

However, hearing the voices so clearly from the other side of the fence gave her pause for thought. It had worried Rose as to how the killer had known that Mary would be at The Croquet club when she was? How had he known her plans?

Hearing the club members voices so clearly made her realize that anyone could have been listening in to any number of conversations from the cemetery. When had Mary and she planned to come for their practise game?

ROSE THOUGHT back to the last time that they were both together at The Croquet Club. It had been on Sunday afternoon.

She could clearly remember Mary laughing at her dreadful game and saying, "Rose, I definitely need to practice before we next play croquet in the tournament," and Rose had replied, "Well, what about 8 a.m. next Wednesday before our 8:45 game? It will give us time to warm up. It always takes me about ten minutes or so to get the feel of the mallet."

With those words Mary's fate had been sealed by the silent listener hidden somewhere in the cemetery.

She turned to Anne and said, "He must have been stalking Mary for a few days, but why did he wait to kill her here?"

Rose was interrupted by Anne pointing to the other side of the cemetery where they could see a man working a weed-whacker around the gravestones.

"Mom, he must be the workman you said you thought Mary knew. Let's go and talk to him," and before Rose could say anything, her impetuous daughter was walking towards the man with a determined step.

"Wait, Anne, wait for me," Rose called as she walked quickly towards the stranger.

He stood about six feet tall, probably in his late fifties, and was clean shaven with dark brown hair. He was handsome in a rugged way.

LOOKING up from his weed whacking, he was obviously startled to see two women coming towards him, although, the young girl in shorts was certainly a welcome sight.

Stopping what he was doing and removing his ear plugs and gloves, he called out, "Is there anything the matter?"

Rose liked the tone of his voice as it was firm but not aggressive.

"Oh, we're sorry to disturb you. I'm Rose Blair and this is my daughter, Anne. I think that you knew my friend Mary."

A cloud of sadness veiled his eyes. He wiped his brow and composed himself.

"Yes, Mary and I were good friends. She would come here to tend to the graves of the children. Come to think of it, she mentioned you quite a lot, buddies you were. It's a nasty business this and it happened here on my turf."

"Had you seen anyone loitering around the cemetery? We think that whoever killed Mary must have stalked her beforehand possibly hiding here in the cemetery while she was playing croquet. Can you think of anyone who was around here a few days before her death?"

The man stood quietly thinking for what seemed like ages. Rose realized that the person before her would never do anything fast. He was a plodder, a turtle, not a hare, but he would get there in the end.

"You know something, there was a man, dark complexioned, had a black beard, I think that he drove a black car although I didn't get to see it properly as he left it parked at the end of the lane."

"What was he doing?"

"Well, I didn't pay too much attention to him at first. We get lots of people popping into the cemetery. Some tourists, but mostly relatives of the departed. Few stay long which is what drew my attention to this man, he seemed to be here for forever. He was just loitering over by the fence near the Croquet Club."

"Um... by the way, what is your name?" Rose asked tentatively.

"It's Michael, Michael Powell. Look, I really liked Mary, but I don't think that I can be much use. The police have already spoken to me. I knew very little about Mary Stokes."

Rose continued undeterred. "But, Michael, why did she tend to the graves of children?"

Michael shuffled his feet and looked uncomfortable.

"Although Mary never talked about her past, I always suspected that she had children of her own somewhere and that they were no longer around.

There was definitely something in her life which haunted her, and my guess is that she lost her kids somehow."

"How dreadful for Mary if she had children and they had died. Oh, dear, Michael, I knew so little about her. It makes me feel so very sad, but what about parents or brothers and sisters? Did she never mention her family?"

"No, but I got the impression that she had no one. They were all dead, just as her whole past seemed dead to her. I thought that it was strange but when I was with Mary, she was always calm and happy, and I just accepted that she didn't want to talk about her past. She was an incredibly private person."

Rose thanked Michael. Anne and she walked back to the car deep in thought. Rose felt quite tearful and hurt that Mary had never confided in her, particularly as they had been such good friends.

They were just about to drive off when Rose looked up and saw a granite headstone bearing the name William Connor.

"Oh, Anne, look, that's where William Connor is buried. He was one of Bayfield's earliest pioneers and an Orange man, one of the youngest Mayors, and quite the leader of men. I've read so much about him in the Historical Society's archives. Do you mind if I look around a bit more before we go home?"

"Of course, I don't mind, Mom. Actually, I think graveyards are rather cool. I'm just going to take some photographs. Take as long as you want." Anne left Rose to wander through the graves.

She came across Maud Stirling's grave. What a woman, to receive the Royal Red Cross for bravery as a nurse in the First World War, was quite the thing. It was also quite amazing to think that she was a schoolteacher in Bayfield first before becoming a nurse and going out to Salonika.

Rose found the Elliott family graves. Those two brothers, Harvey and Fred, and that awful murder.

Poor Mrs. Elliott, Rose thought as she walked along the graves reading the inscriptions as she went. The Erwin's, the Gairdner's, Tudor Marks, the MacLeod's, the Baileys, the list went on and on of names that Rose was familiar with through the history of Bayfield.

Anne joined her at the car, and they drove back in silence both deep in thought.

"You know something, Mom," Anne said as they neared their house. "I've been thinking about your friend, Mary.

When I moved to Halifax, I wanted a new life, a fresh start away from Seth and Toronto and, indeed all the unhappiness I associated with living there. I can understand her wanting to create a new life, but she must have had parents or brothers and sisters of her own that she would miss and would surely want to stay in contact. You need to find out what happened to her family in order to understand what was going on in her life."

Rose thought of the photograph by the side of Mary's bed that she had seen and how Mary had said rather too quickly that it was her sister and children in the photograph. The picture had shown a woman who looked just like Mary, admittedly a younger Mary, and a handsome man with his arms around her shoulders. Two adorable children stood in front of, presumably, their parents, a little girl and a little boy. What if the photo was actually of Mary and her family and not the sister as she had claimed?

They pulled into the driveway and Anne fairly jumped out ahead calling out to Alan. She fairly leapt into his arms when he appeared smiling at the door. He gave her a big kiss and Anne excitedly told him all about the cemetery and the meeting with Michael Powell.

"It's so cool there, Alan, not in the least bit creepy. I took tons of photographs. We think that Mary, Mom's friend, had a husband and children and that they are all dead."

"So how does that help you with finding her murderer?" Alan said as he untangled himself from Anne's embrace and went to sit down.

Rose came in and said, "No more talk of Mary. Let's go out for lunch and then Tom wants to take you both for a sail this afternoon. Where do you fancy going to eat?"

In the end they decided to eat at The Red Pump. Sitting outside on the rear patio under an umbrella, the fountain tinkling in the background, Rose was transported back to Europe where they seemed to do nothing but spend endless hours under umbrellas at cafes drinking wine or coffee. It was a good life.

Without being able to stop it, a flashback to that coffee shop in Vienna flew through Rose's mind. Jim Reynolds with a woman who looked very much like her friend Susan Parker and how they had both crept out of the café before their order had been served and then the indecision over who to contact?

Neither of them knew how to speak German. How could they explain to the police who Jim Reynolds was?

Tom had finally suggested that they go back to their hotel and use the internet and email Susan. She would know how to contact the European authorities.

They had done just that, only they had both felt bad. Had they contacted the Austrian Police straight away Jim Reynolds would probably have been caught.

"Mom, Mom," Anne called breaking Rose's reverie. "Are you alright?"

"Yes, of course I am, dear. I was just remembering our trip last year to Vienna and how we often sat outside under umbrellas like this. The Red Pump patio has just a very European feel about it."

Their lunch arrived and the next hour was spent eating a delicious meal and generally enjoying the magic of good food with family and friends.

SUSAN CAME out of the spa feeling quite relaxed. She looked at her watch and gasped. It was almost three o'clock. There would still be time, however, to drive out to the cemetery and interview Michael Powell, the grounds keeper.

Five minutes later she had parked her car at the top of the gravel lane entrance to the cemetery. Susan got out of her car and looked around. It was a beautiful cemetery, very tranquil and hard to believe that a brutal murder had taken place there just one week ago.

She could see no sign of Michael Powell. After walking around, it was obvious that he was nowhere to be found. He must have gone home, Susan thought as she got back into her car. Goshen Line was only five minutes away. It would be an easy drive to his trailer.

Susan turned onto Goshen Line and immediately noticed a huge plume of black smoke mushrooming into the sky.

Her heart lurched. It looked to be coming from behind a farmhouse. She pulled her car over and grabbed her cell phone.

Punching in 911 she alerted the fire department and police even though technically she was the police. Susan had just finished her call, when a black Mercedes came tearing past her.

She had no time to give chase as she had reached the source of the smoke. The trailer was totally ablaze. Huge, ugly, flames were flaring out of the windows.

A car was parked in the driveway, presumably belonging to

Michael. Susan jumped out of her car screaming out Michael's name. Without stopping to think she opened the trailer door.

There was an almighty blast, and she was blown backwards with such force that she landed at least ten metres away from the burning trailer. Susan couldn't remember what happened afterwards because the next thing she knew was waking up in a hospital bed, a drip in her hand and bandages all over her arms.

INSPECTOR HENRI LE BRUIN was the first person that she saw when she regained consciousness.

Standing in the doorway carrying a huge bouquet of flowers he stood looking as handsome as ever.

Wearing a pale blue shirt with his sleeves rolled up, light tanned pants, and his sun-bleached hair still slightly longer than most of his counterparts. He wore a frown of worry across his normally sunny face.

The nurse came in carrying a vase for the flowers and asked if Susan needed anything. Henri stepped forward and tenderly kissed her on her forehead.

"*Ma cherie*, you had us all worried. How do you feel?"

Susan smiled. She actually didn't feel bad at all, just a bit groggy. She looked down at her bandaged arms. "What happened to my arms?" she said.

Henri told her that she had cuts and scratches and one particularly nasty gash, but miraculously she had narrowly missed being burnt.

"The force of the explosion blew you backwards as far as the farmhouse."

"What about the owner of the trailer, Michael Powell?" Susan asked with trepidation.

Henri went quiet for a moment. "I'm afraid that he didn't make it. Actually, the forensic team's initial report shows contusions to the back of his head consistent with a blow to the head. We think that he was almost certainly unconscious, if not dead, before the fire ignited the whole trailer."

"Henri, I saw that black Mercedes when I was heading over to the trailer. Do you have any more information on the vehicle?"

Henri kissed Susan again and told her to stop worrying, she should rest. They were still looking into the Serbian Syndicate and would have more information by the end of the day.

"The good news is, *ma cherie*, they are going to discharge you tomorrow morning, providing someone will be around to care for you while you rest. No work for you for a few days at least. I said that I could take care of you for three days until I have to be back in Montreal."

Susan smiled weakly. The thought of Henri caring for her was actually rather appealing. She was glad that she had that bikini wax and pedicure.

"What about the investigation?" Susan asked having been jolted back into reality at the thought of work.

"Don't worry, *cherie*, I'm happy to assist while I'm here in Bayfield but you have a competent team. Sergeant Flowers has already brought me up to date on everything. Besides, I have a fair bit of information to share regarding the black Mercedes. Also, I hate to concern you with this while you're still recovering from the explosion but our friend, Jim Reynolds, is back on the radar. Interpol contacted us to say that they had been watching a Dutch man, Gert Bruisma, who they believe to be part of a smuggling outfit and the customs officers in Turkey have just confirmed that Gert Bruisma and Jim Reynolds are the same person. It seems that our man is up to his old tricks again."

Susan sighed. She had never told Henri how intimately she had known Jim Reynolds. If truth be known, she was horribly embarrassed by the whole affair.

How could she, a police officer, have not known what he was up to when it was right under her nose. Susan cringed at the thought of the relationship that had lasted for over a year.

Henri kissed her goodbye and said that he would be back first thing in the morning. Susan lay back against the pillow, closed her eyes and tried to blank out that last image she had of the trailer going up in flames.

TOM TOOK Anne and Alan off for an afternoon sail leaving Rose to prepare the evening meal and to spend some time with Ben and Puff.

She hated to leave the dogs alone for too long. They suffered from separation anxiety, well, maybe it was Rose who just didn't want to be away from her beloved pets too long.

Already it felt as if Puff had been part of their family forever.

She got out the ingredients to make the lemon meringue pie.

First, she had to zest the lemons, squeeze out the juice, then separate the eggs, and add those to the lemon juice. A tablespoon of corn starch and sugar were added and then the whole mixture was cooked over a saucepan of water to prevent the egg yolks from curdling.

She poured the lemon curd into the pie crust, whisked up the egg whites with some sugar and spooned the meringue on top of the lemon. Rose always liked to cook her lemon meringue pie slowly in a low oven so that the meringue would end up being crispy and not spongy like some of the pies that she had eaten.

While she had the lemons out, Rose decided to make up a batch of Tom's favourite Lemon Squares. They were really easy to make and Tom simply adored them.

Having made the desserts, she turned to the Moussaka. Collecting all the ingredients, ground mince, onion, garlic, tomato paste, eggplant, and potatoes she proceeded to make the meat sauce. Slicing up the potatoes she put those onto cook and then sliced up the eggplant and let that roast in the oven while the pie was cooking.

Finally, Rose layered the meat sauce alternatively with the sliced potatoes and eggplant ending up with a layer of potatoes.

She then quickly made a cheese sauce which she poured over the top and put the finished Moussaka to one side. She would bake it 40 minutes before they were ready to eat their dinner.

Rose had just made herself a cup of tea and was about to sit down in the sunroom and relax for a while when the telephone rang. It was Tom. They had just finished sailing and were going to pop into the Docks for a quick drink before coming home.

They would be back by 5:30 p.m.

Rose thanked Tom for letting her know and then she looked at her watch. It was 4:30 p.m. If she put the Moussaka in the oven at 5:15 pm they would be ready to eat by 6:00 pm. Perfect. She had one hour to herself. It was time to catch up on some reading.

She belonged to a couple of book clubs in the village. Indeed, it always made people gasp when Rose told them that Bayfield had over 16 book clubs.

In fact, the village bookshop regularly arranged for popular authors to come and give talks about their books.

Rose and Tom had been to quite a few *Books and Brunch* events usually held at The Little Inn, and they had all been fabulous.

Her next book club was to be held at Becky's house and it was coming up fast. Next Tuesday, in fact, and Rose had not even started the book, *Life of Pi,* by Jan Martel.

Fortunately, she had read it several years before shortly after the book had first been published. She still remembered being absolutely shocked to discover that Richard Parker, a character in the book, was actually a tiger.

Other than the tiger, Rose could barely remember the story, but she did know how much she had enjoyed it. She read so many books and had trouble remembering which book it was that she had read the month before, let alone one from a few years back.

That was truly one of the aspects that she didn't like about getting old. The 'spongy' brain. Rose thought, *I never, ever, had trouble in remembering things when I was younger.*

She often had the same conversation with her friends and at least they were all in the same boat, which was a consolation of sorts.

The afternoon sun sent dappled rays of light into the sunroom where Rose sat curled up with her book, Ben and Puff at her feet. She was just enjoying her second cup of tea when the telephone rang. It was Paul from Japan.

Rose glanced at her watch. It would be 5 a.m. in Japan. Alarm bells went off in her head.

"Paul, Paul, is everything ok?"

There was a pause and then Paul cried, "Mom, it's Atsuko. She was rushed into hospital last night with a burst appendix. Oh, Mom, it was dreadful." There was another pause and a cough, and then Paul continued with a voice thick with emotion.

"Peritonitis, the doctors said. Mom, I thought that she wasn't going to make it." There was another long pause and cough.

Rose said quietly, "Darling, how is she now?"

"She's in intensive care but the doctors say that she is strong and providing that the antibiotics kick in she will be okay. Oh, Mom, it was so awful."

"Well, love, it doesn't sound as if you've slept much. Why don't you go to bed and get some sleep, and by the time that you wake up I reckon that Atsuko will be much better. There is nothing that you can do now. She needs to let the antibiotics do their work."

"Oh, but I want to be at her bedside when she wakes up."

Rose said quietly, "But darling, she hopefully will sleep for a good six to eight hours or so. If you don't get any sleep, you won't be any use to anyone. Go home and ask the hospital to call you the minute that she stirs."

"Mom, you're probably right. I am dog tired. By the way, Atsuko and I think that we might come home for Christmas. Would that be alright?"

"Oh, darling, that would be great. Abby and Ella will be thrilled. But can you get the time off work?"

"Yes, I have two weeks off at Christmas. The school is closed for that period."

Paul had been taken on at a Canadian Maple Leaf School to teach English three days a week.

The rest of the week was spent teaching English to employees of the Toyota plant.

"What about the businessmen who you teach at Toyota?"

"Well, as long as I let them know in advance, I can just cancel those classes. Atsuko is between jobs right now. She's working from home."

Atsuko had studied fashion design at the University of Tokyo.

She designed her own wedding dresses, one for the Japanese wedding and one for the Canadian wedding. Rose had seen some of her sketches for a line of children's clothing and they were perfect.

She had suggested that she had some clothes made up and sent to Jessica. Abby and Ella could model the clothes and surely get some orders for her.

Atsuko had said that she was hoping that a fashion house would be interested in her designs and then they would pay for the commercial production of the outfits.

Young people are so savvy, Rose thought as she put the phone down having concluded her conversation with Paul.

She hadn't really thought about Christmas. In the middle of summer, Christmas always seemed light years away yet every year it seemed to creep up to them way too quickly.

Jessica had talked about 'doing' Christmas at their house this year and Rose, who had always cooked the turkey and done the whole traditional thing, wasn't quite sure what to think.

At some point having one's own Christmas lunch was like a rite of passage and was all part of growing up. She and Tom had always taken it in turns to have Christmas day at either one or the other of their parents until Jessica, Paul, and Anne one Christmas said that they didn't want to go to Nana's house.

They wanted to stay at home for Christmas, and that was when their own tradition had started.

Mind you, Jessica was about twelve then and Abby and Ella were still young enough to go along with their parents plans without questioning.

If Jessica and Rob were ready to embrace the whole family Christmas, then far be it for Rose to object.

Actually, the more that she thought about it the better it sounded. Cooking the Christmas turkey with all the trimmings had to be Rose's least favourite meal to prepare.

She always did the same meal well at Thanksgiving so at least this would be one less turkey to have to cook.

At 5:30 p.m. Tom, Anne, and Alan returned, and her peace was shattered by Anne calling out, "Mom, Mom, you'll never guess what! That nice man, Michael, died in a house fire and your friend, Inspector Parker, was injured trying to save him."

"What..." Rose said barely believing her ears.

Tom entered the kitchen and kissed Rose on her cheek. "Yes, I'm afraid Anne's right, love. It was all the talk of the pub. It happened earlier on this afternoon around 3:00 p.m."

Rose looked shocked. "That's dreadful. We were only talking to him this morning, Anne and I. Oh, that quite upset me."

Tom put his arms around Rose and gave her a hug.

"It looks like Susan, is going to be okay. She was blown backwards away from the fire by the force of the explosion."

"It all sounds horrific. First Mary, and now this. What is happening to our sleepy village?

Oh, I forgot. Anne, Tom, Paul phoned. Atsuko is in hospital with a burst appendix. Paul sounded very upset, poor darling."

Tom nodded sagely. "It's awful when something as sudden as an appendix ruptures. It happened to my father and we almost lost him."

Anne clapped her hands. "Enough of this misery everyone. Mom, do you want Alan and I to lay the table?"

Rose jumped up. Dinner, she had completely forgotten to put the moussaka in the oven. They would just have to wait and eat their dinner a bit later.

"Yes, darling, if you don't mind laying the table that would be great. Tom, can you pour me a stiff drink. I think I need one."

EIGHT

Henri Le Bruin arrived at Goderich hospital right at 8:00 a.m. Normally patients were not discharged before 11:00 a.m. but as Susan only had cuts on her arms and her concussion had been fifteen hours ago, she was free to go. Henri escorted her to his car, and they drove off to The Bayfield Village Inn and her bedroom suite.

"Susan, cheri, I'll just see you comfortable and then I will go and meet up with your team at The Lion's Hall. I'll be back at lunch time and we'll go out to eat then. Will you be alright on your own?"

"Oh, Henri, I'm not an invalid you know, but I will rest up just for this one day but then I will need to get back to work. Come here, my love, and give me a kiss."

Henri encircled Susan with his long arms and before they knew it, both were on the bed tearing at each other's clothes in a fever of passion.

It had been a long time since either of them had made love. Afterwards Susan laughed. So much for her being an invalid. If anything her body had not felt so alive and invigorated in a long time.

Half an hour later, after an invigorating shower, Susan was

tucked up in bed and Henri was on his way to The Lion's Hall where he was to meet the whole investigation team.

Sergeant Flowers greeted the Inspector formally and introduced the others in the team.

"Listen up, everyone. Inspector Le Bruin is from the Surete Crimes Unit in Montreal. He had been looking into the black Mercedes for us. Before he takes the floor, I have an email to share from forensics.

It is conclusive that Michael Powell was dead before the trailer caught fire. There was no smoke inhalation in his lungs. So, we are definitely looking at murder.

I also have a note from the fire chief. It appears that the fire was started with gasoline. In other words, we are looking at arson. I think that we can say that it is too much of a coincidence that the black Mercedes was seen leaving the property just before the fire ignited. We now have our prime suspect identified. Over to you Inspector."

Henri took the floor. He had prepared a short PowerPoint presentation.

Clicking on his computer, a picture of a swarthy, bearded man came up on the screen.

"This, gentlemen, is Ljuba Strugar, one of Serbia's top hit men. He is basically a hired assassin, ruthless and extremely dangerous.

We can now implicate him for the murder of Michael Powell and, I believe, that he tried to run Rose and Tom Blair over when they were out walking their dogs.

It could be, too, that he is also Mary Stokes' assassin as the crossbow is one of his trademarks. Now when was the last sighting of the black Mercedes before yesterday?"

Sergeant Flowers stood up and flicked through his notebook.

"Let me see. Yes, I have it here. Mrs. Blair reported being followed by a black Mercedes from Goderich to the O.P.P. detachment station, just on the south of the town.

She was so frightened that she had the common sense to pull into the police station and ask for help.

This same vehicle was seen parked outside Tim Horton's in Goderich and the driver fits the description we have of Ljuba."

"Merci, Constable. Anyone else to report further sightings of the Mercedes?"

Constable Elliot stood up. "Well, when we spoke to Michael Powell, he said that he had seen what looked like a black car pull away from the cemetery a couple of days before Mary Stokes was murdered.

Then, of course, it was seen again by Mr. Blair cruising around the Square when she was with her grandchildren at the Bayfield splash pad. Oh, yes, there was also one more sighting in Seaforth.

A security camera picked up this grainy picture of a bearded man filling up a black Mercedes with gas at the Shell station." He showed the Inspector the photograph.

"Merci, Constable. Ljuba is obviously still at large in the community. Now, moving on to the mysterious Pierre La Ville, the man flagged on Mary Stokes' computer contact list. I've run his name through all the Quebec data bases and every time his name comes up blocked.

Finally, I found out why his name has been constantly inaccessible to the public and that is because he works as a Federal agent. In what capacity, I do not know, but we were able to ascertain the reason for the flag and it is only a matter of time before we get to the bottom of this.

Unfortunately, anything Federal has to go through so much red tape. I'm afraid it won't happen quickly. Sergeant, do you have anything to add?"

Sergeant Flowers was just about to speak when the phone rang. He answered it immediately.

"Yes... black Mercedes, Winthrop Line. Thank you."

He put the phone down and turned to the team.

"You have probably gathered from my brief conversation that the black Mercedes has been found abandoned on Winthrop Line, just North of Seaforth."

Henri stood up and walked over to where a map of Huron County hung on the wall. He traced his finger to Seaforth and then found Winthrop Line.

"Eh bien, our man has abandoned his car in the middle of nowhere. He must have arranged to have another vehicle available or someone to pick him up. We can assume that he is still in the area. Has his photograph been shown around?"

Constable Brown answered, "Yes, sir. We had the photograph from the garage enlarged. Although it is quite grainy and his face is clear. It's the beard and general swarthiness that gives him away.

Of course, if he was clean shaven, he would be much harder to identify. Constable Elliot and I have shown this around the community and so far, sightings have been quite plentiful."

Constable Brown pulled out his notebook and began to read.

"Yesterday at 9 a.m. at Tim Horton's in Clinton, Sunset Diner around 12.15 p.m., The Albion, 6 p.m. Our man has been tracked through his eating habits."

"Bon, merci, Constable Brown. Keep showing his photo around the community. Now team, there is a known ruthless killer lose in this area.

He has to be apprehended and fast before he kills again. Inspector Parker mentioned to me that you were watching the Blair home because of the stalking.

I want you to increase the surveillance. Ljuba is a hired assassin working under strict orders to eliminate certain targets.

In this case we already have two people assassinated, two people connected to by a relationship that they were having.

Is Rose Blair another target? And if so, why? We need to maintain a strict surveillance at all times on the Blair property. This man is extremely dangerous. He is a professional killer and will stop at nothing."

TOM COOKED breakfast for all of them. He liked frying up bacon and eggs but left the scones and baking to Rose. Today she was making cranberry and lemon scones. There was some homemade peach jam in the fridge which would go very well with the scones. Over breakfast Tom suggested that Anne and Alan go for a walk on the Saw Mill Creek Trail.

"I'll come with you and we can take the dogs. They could do with a nice, long walk." He said while munching on some toast. With that decided, they finished their breakfast, helped clear away the dishes and were out of the house by ten, leaving Rose to a few hours of peace. She had just finished cleaning the kitchen when the telephone rang. It was Susan Parker.

"Rose, I promised that I would rest up today but I'm quite frankly bored. Do you fancy coming over for coffee here at The Bayfield Village Inn?"

Rose looked at her watch. She had planned to prepare lunch, a quiche and salad, but friends always came first in her book and it wasn't often that Susan called and invited her for coffee.

"Yes, I'd love to but only for about an hour as I have loads to do here. See you in five minutes."

Rose rushed to their bedroom, brushed her hair, and freshened up her lipstick and grabbed her purse. Five minutes later she had parked her car and was entering the foyer of the Bayfield Village Inn.

Susan was seated in the lounge. A fresh pot of coffee and two cups and saucers had been set on the table. Rose looked around. "This is lovely. You know something, I've driven past this place hundreds of times before but never been inside."

"There is a great indoor swimming pool, Rose. I like staying here because I just love to swim. Unfortunately, because of the cuts on my arms, I have to refrain from swimming for a few days which is a real shame."

Susan poured out the coffee and handed a cup to Rose.

"How much longer do you think that you'll be here, Susan?" Rose asked as she poured some cream into her coffee.

"That's a very good question, my friend. We still have a murder to solve although I feel it in my bones that we are closing in on our killer. Henri, umm... I mean Inspector Le Bruin, from the Montreal Major Crimes Unit, has a name for our killer. He is apparently a Serbian hit man and a trained assassin, very ruthless and dangerous.

So... we have a name but still no motive. Normally hit men are mercenaries who will contract out to anyone willing to pay enough. We're not sure about this Serb. He is connected to the Serbian Syndicate in Montreal, very, very strongly tied to the Serb-Montenegrin forces way back in the 90's in the days of President Milosevic.

The Montreal Major Crimes unit has a whole dossier on gangland attacks mostly on the Croatians living in the city. That was primarily in the 1990s but recently there has been a resurgence of unrest amongst the Serbians and the Croatians in the city.

How all of this connects to Mary Stokes and Michael Powell, we have yet to find out?"

Rose was thoughtful.

"You know something, Susan. I think that Mary had a whole family that was somehow wiped out during that awful war. Maybe they were somehow involved with this Serbian fraction in Montreal. I don't know, but something Michael Powell said to me about Mary tending to the graves of children, struck a chord.

That photograph, you know, the one and only photograph in Mary's house showing a young couple with two children, well I believe that was a picture of her very own family."

Susan looked at Rose with amazement. "You mean to tell me that you went out to the cemetery and spoke to Michael Powell? When was that?"

Rose told Susan how Anne and she had driven out and spoken to Michael.

"You were probably the last person to see him alive.

He spoke to a couple of my Constables the previous day, although he never mentioned the bit about Mary tending to the children's graves."

Rose sighed audibly before replying.

"He was a sensitive, deep thinking man, Michael, and I do believe Mary and he shared some happiness together. I still am amazed at how secretive she was. I feel a bit slighted to think that we were such good friends and she never trusted me enough to tell me about her life or her affair with Michael."

Susan patted Rose's shoulder. "Oh, I wouldn't feel upset, Rose. It's just some people's coping skills are to keep everything contained within themselves. She obviously had a past that she was determined to forget. You were her present, her fresh, new start, her best friend."

"Thank you, Susan. Well, on that note I had better get going. Anne, Alan, and Tom will be back soon, and I need to get lunch started."

"Oh, Rose, you're always cooking. Send them out for lunch or go and pick up some Subway sandwiches."

Rose looked shocked. She would never dream of serving take-out food to guests, but it did get her thinking.

"I suppose that I could call into Foodland and pick up a cooked chicken and serve that with a nice salad."

"There you go, Rose, you're taking a leaf out of my book. I never cook unless I really have to."

Rose laughed and gave her friend a hug.

"You haven't changed a bit my friend. Remember all those Chinese take-always you bought when it was your turn to cook at university?"

They both laughed, remembering the heady days at Queen's

University in Kingston where they had both shared a house and Rose, even all those years ago had insisted on cooking proper meals.

As Rose drove out of The Bayfield Village Inn car park, she noticed a dark, blue car pulled up behind her. The driver had a black beard and made Rose's heart miss a beat, however, as she turned right onto Short Hill the blue car kept driving ahead. *I'm being silly and jumpy*, Rose thought as she pulled into their drive.

It was strangely quiet entering their house without the normal barking from Ben and Puff. Rose put her purse down on the countertop and then suddenly remembered that she was supposed to be picking up a cooked chicken for their lunch and had completely forgotten.

Oh well, she thought, back to the original plan of making quiche for lunch. She set to making the pastry.

Getting out her trusted food processor Rose zipped up the pastry and then began to roll it out.

Afterwards, she couldn't remember what had made her walk to the front window, but she did and to her horror the same dark, blue car that had been following her, now sat in their driveway.

She saw the shadow of a man standing in front of the front door.

Fortunately, the front door was self-locking, but not the back door. Rose rushed over to the rear door and turned the dead lock.

She knew that locking their doors would barely deter the killer, but it might just give her some time. Rose grabbed the phone and pushed in 911. After giving her address to the operator she blurted out "Please come quickly, a man is trying to kill me."

Rose then phoned Susan. "Susan, that assassin is here trying to break in. I've called 911 but they may take ages to get here. What should I do?"

"Rose, listen to me. You have to either get out or hide. Believe me this man will stop at nothing to kill you. Now go, go now."

Rose looked at the front door. Could she unlock it and escape without him hearing? The decision was made for her when the back window crashed open scattering a million pieces of glass to the kitchen floor. A hand appeared and that galvanized Rose into action.

She ran to the hall closet. Inside there were all their winter coats and boots. Rose closed the door quietly behind her and pushed herself up against the back of the closet hiding her body behind all the coats.

Her heart was beating so fast and loudly that it sounded to her like a stampede of horses. Rose held her breath. She could hear footsteps in the hallway and doors being opened. *Please God*, Rose thought, *protect me from this monster."*

Suddenly the closet door was yanked open and Rose could feel the coats being pushed on their hangers to one side as he searched inside.

She squeezed her body tightly up against the wall just hoping that she would be hidden in the shadows of the back of the closet.

Afterwards she swore that he had just set eyes on her when the police sirens could be heard louder and louder and then the front door was smashed in and the killer bolted back through the kitchen.

The next thing Rose heard was a gun shot and then silence followed by what sounded like a whole army of people running through the house. She remained hidden. Then she heard Susan calling out her name and it was only then that Rose shakily came out of the closet.

"Oh, Rose, thank God you're safe." And Rose rushed into Susan's arms and burst into tears.

"They got him you know. You don't have to worry anymore."

Tom, Anne, Alan, and the dogs arrived back soon afterwards and in shocked silence they surveyed the scene before them. The front door lay flat on the floor and the back window was completely smashed to smithereens.

There was some activity going on in the yard and Tom went to go and have a look when Susan put a firm hand on his shoulder and said,

"Don't go outside, Tom. The ambulance will be here soon to take away the body but it's not a pretty sight.

Why don't you make your wife a cup of tea? I think that she really needs one right now."

Later that day when the police had all left and Tom had fixed the front door and duct taped a sheet of plastic over the smashed window, Rose sat in the sun lounge with Alan and Tom while Anne pottered in the kitchen making them all dinner.

Alan said while holding a beer in his hand, "Is it always as crazy as this in Bayfield?" and Rose and Tom smiled and said together, "Not always, just sometimes!"

NINE

Susan got up quietly and put on her swimming costume. She was dying for a swim. The cuts on her arm were healing nicely, they would be fine.

She crept out of the room not wanting to wake Henri up. He was sleeping like a baby, gently snoring and looking as snug as a bug in a rug.

Susan dived gracefully into the beautiful pool and thirty laps later she had towel dried her wet body and was back in bed with Henri.

Snuggling up to his hot body he wrapped his arms around her and drew her into him. Before long they were making deep, passionate love.

That's the way to start the day, Susan thought later while she was in the shower. It saddened her to think that Henri would be leaving that day. They were so good together, had the right chemistry, but it was just the long distance away from each other that had previously impacted their relationship.

Susan knew that to make it work either she would have to move to Montreal or Henri move to London. Last year she had toyed with the idea of retirement but if truth be known she was a bit afraid of not working.

Yet Tom and Rose were both retired, and they always seemed busy and happy, maybe it was different for couples, but living on her own and not working simply terrified her.

"Ma, cheri, when will we see each other again?" Henri was in the shower with his arms around her. He moved to kiss her deeply before she could reply.

Susan broke away from his embrace and said, "I'll have to look at my schedule, Henri. This investigation is still open. Although we have the murderer, we still have not discovered the motive. Ljuba was just the awful messenger. We have to find whom he worked for.

When you get any further information on Pierre La Ville that might help us to fill in some of the blanks in Mary Stokes life, let me know as soon as possible. I still feel that her past holds the key to all of this."

"As soon as I hear anything more about Pierre La Ville, I will send it on to you *tout suite*. But stop talking business, come here, I want to caress your lovely body."

Thirty minutes later Susan and Henri departed both with smiles on their faces.

The team was all assembled, the coffee on. There was a general buzz of excitement in the air.

"Good morning, everyone. Firstly, I want to congratulate you all on a job well done. You worked together as a team and as a result, we got our man.

However, our investigation is by no means closed. We may have our murderer, but we are still no wiser as to the motive and why our victims were chosen. So, let us continue to dig. Rose Blair has a theory that our Mary Stokes once had a family and that they were all killed.

Turning to her Sergeant Susan continued, "Sergeant Flowers can you look into deaths occurring before 1996. We know that she married Graham Stokes in 1998 and that she had a driver's license issued in 1996 but we have no record of her life before 1996. Look up deaths of a father and two children under the name of Watson, Mary's name before she married Graham Stokes. Constable Elliot, can you look into Michael Powell's background. I want his whole life story. Hopefully that will be reasonably easy to piece together. There is an ex-wife somewhere. You will need to find and interview her. Constable Mathieson, any joy in finding where Ljuba was staying?"

"Sorry, ma'am, we're still making enquiries, however, we did find a whole arsenal of weapons in the trunk of his car. Everything is being catalogued right now but we should have a complete list by tomorrow."

"Was there any personal I.D. on his body or in the car?"

"No, absolutely nothing. If Inspector Le Bruin had not run his name through the Quebec database, we would have been dealing with a complete mystery man."

"Well, he was on contract and working for someone and it is our job to find out whom. Sergeant, keep the lines of communication going with the Montreal division. Somehow the Serbian syndicate has to be tied up with all of this. Right, men, keep digging. I need to go and visit Rose Blair and get a full statement from her. See you all tomorrow."

The officers all left the room leaving Susan deep in thought.

TOM WAS GOING to drive Anne and Alan to London to visit Jessica, Rob, and the girls before they flew back to Halifax. As they were getting ready to leave Anne came up to her mother and said, "Mom, are you sure that you'll be alright? You look ever so pale."

It was true. Rose had got up and looked in the bathroom mirror only to be shocked by what she saw. Not only did she look as pale as a ghost, but she had great, dark shadows beneath her eyes.

I look ancient, she thought as she hurriedly applied some concealer and foundation cream to her face.

Tom came up and gave Rose a big hug. "Are you sure you're okay, love?"

"Oh, yes, you two, I'm perfectly fine. Oh, but I'm going to miss you, Anne. Look after the baby. Dad and I will try to fly out soon to visit you and I'll definitely be out for the birth in February. Just stay well and happy my darling."

To Alan Rose said, "Take care of our daughter, Alan, she is very precious to us." Rose gave him a big hug.

Puff and Ben came to say their goodbyes too. With the luggage, dogs tails wagging, then Anne crying, Rose felt as if she would also burst into tears if they didn't hurry up and depart.

By the time Tom set off, Rose was ready for a strong cup of tea. She made a pot, buttered a ginger and orange scone and took her tea and a plate of scones over to the sunroom.

It was another glorious day. The sky was a stunning blue. A bright red cardinal perched on one of the pear trees and two hummingbirds were buzzing around the honeysuckle.

The garden was looking particularly good that year. Large terra-cotta pots filled with crimson red geraniums framed the patio and a salmon pink climbing rose bush cascaded over a lattice screen Tom had made for the garden.

A blue jay plopped down into the bird bath. *Life was so good,* Rose thought as she snuggled up on the sofa with Ben and Puff determined to get The *Life of Pi* finished before her book club on Tuesday. But it was not to be, because the phone rang and shattered her peace abruptly.

"Rose speaking. Oh, Susan, how nice to hear you. Yes, come on over. I've got tea already made and some orange and ginger scones just waiting for you."

Ten minutes later Susan was sitting in the sunroom sipping tea with Rose.

"So how do you feel today, Rose?"

"To be honest I feel a bit shaky still. I suppose it is delayed shock or something. I keep thinking how I could have been killed. I still don't know why though?"

"Believe me, Rose, we're not going to stop this investigation until we have found out why. No, what you're actually suffering from is post-traumatic stress disorder, PTSD it's called. It will pass but if you find that you're not sleeping or have any other lasting symptoms, you must seek medical advice."

"Oh, I'll be okay, Susan, although I don't think that I will be able to rest easy until we find out the whole story. It all just seems so bizarre. There is one thing that has been playing on my mind, though and that is that Mary hasn't been laid to rest. There has been no funeral."

Susan put her tea down and said, "We haven't released the body because we had hoped to find a relative to release it to. Did you want to organize a small funeral?"

Rose nodded her head, "Susan, that is the very least that I could do.

If the police can arrange for a cremation, I'll organize a Memorial Service at The Town Hall.

When can you realistically have the body interred?"

"A couple of days would do it. I'll get on to the morgue straight away, but you could go ahead with the service regardless of the cremation?"

"Yes, you're right. It will feel far more like closure having a service. I do wish though, that we knew more about Mary's past life?"

"Rose, we're getting there, slowly, piecing together the fragments of her life. Now I must first take a full statement from you. I didn't tell you yesterday, but the man was armed with a crossbow.

It was only when he let one of the bolts fly at one of our officers that he was shot. By the way, I would like to come to the memorial service. Just let me know when you've sorted out the details."

Susan spent the next ten minutes taking a formal statement from Rose and then she got up to leave. Ben and Puff jumped off the sofa and followed her to the front door.

"Tom fixed this well," Susan remarked as she opened the door, "It just needs a little touch up paint. You know that you can invoice the police department for compensation?"

"Oh, it's nothing. We're just pleased that the door wasn't actually broken. I've got a new sheet of glass being installed later on this afternoon and then the house will be as right as rain again."

Rose gave Susan a hug and closed the door behind her. She went back to the sunroom, grabbed a writing pad and pen and proceeded to write up a guest list for Mary's memorial. She would email the invitations out after booking the Town Hall.

Tom returned from London later on that afternoon. He had eaten lunch at Jessica's and had played ball with Abby and Ella in the garden. The girls wouldn't stop talking about Puff.

"Did you tell Jessica about yesterday?" Rose hoped that Tom had not said a word as their daughter was a worrier and would have been shocked had she known about the assassin.

"Well, no, I didn't but Anne blurted it out the minute that we got there. Jessica was horrified. She wants us to move to London. She thinks that Bayfield is too dangerous a place to live."

"Oh, Tom, I hope that you reassured her that we are fine and actually, I do feel fine now. Susan came over and we talked. I'm going to organize a memorial service for Mary. That should put some closure on the whole sorry business."

"There you go again, love, organizing everything, but yes, I think that's a good idea having a service however, who are you going to invite? She didn't have many friends."

"Well, there are the Croquet Club members and the Fitness Class ladies. Even though no one knew her very well people will still come just out of respect. I've booked the Town Hall for tomorrow."

"Crikey, Rose, you don't beat about the bush do you love? Is there anything that I can do?" Before Rose could answer, the telephone rang.

"Umm... hello. You don't know me, but I was a friend of Mary Stokes and she often talked about you. I believe that she passed away last week. I was wondering if I could meet with you soon as I'm in this area for a few days."

Rose thought quickly. She had booked the Town Hall for 2:00 p.m. Maybe he would like to come to the service and they could talk afterwards. He agreed and she was about to put the phone down when Rose suddenly realized that she had not got his name.

"Oh, excuse me. I didn't get your name?"

"Of course, it's Pierre La Ville..."

TEN

"Good morning everyone. Before we give our reports, I want to let you all know that there is a Memorial Service for Mary Stokes at 2:00 p.m. today to be held at The Town Hall. It would be nice if some of you could attend. I will be going myself. Sergeant Flowers, have you anything to report on the investigation of the possible death of the Watson family?"

Sergeant Flowers stood up and shook his head saying: "No, ma'am. There are no records of any deaths of a father and two children under the name of Watson either before 1996 or after. Sorry, I drew a complete blank. "

"Oh, well, it was just a possible theory. Constable Elliot, what did you find out about Michael Powell?"

Constable Elliot drew out his notebook and began to read in a rather monotone voice.

"He was born in 1961 in Sarnia. Went to school at St. Claire Secondary School. Left school at age 16, worked at odd jobs for ten years, no specific training. Married Elaine Dent in 1984. They had two children, two boys, Ian and Joe. They moved to Exeter where

Elaine's family lived. Divorced one year later. That is about it, ma'am. A pretty average sort of life."

"When was he taken on by the municipality?"

The Constable looked at his notes again.

"In 2009, ma'am. He's been with them for almost five years now. I spoke to the clerk over in Zurich and she said that he was a good worker, no complaints."

"Thank you, Constable Elliot. Constable Mathieson, anymore on Ljuba Strugar?"

"Yes, ma'am. I received this email from the Montreal Division yesterday evening. Ljuba Strugar appeared to live in Verdun. He leaves a wife and two children who have not seen him for one month.

They emigrated from Serbia twenty years ago when he was a young man of eighteen. His wife knows nothing about his activities.

She was under the understanding that he worked in imports and exports and knew nothing about any gangland fighting I have a full copy of her statement here and will copy you all in."

"Thank you, Constable. Well, team, we are slowly closing in. It looks as if the Stokes family can be eliminated from the enquiry. George had no motive to murder his stepmother. There also appears to be no reason why Michael Powell was murdered and the same could be said of the attempted murder of Rose Blair. What they both have in common is a connection to Mary Stokes. Could it be a case of murder by association? Possibly, but we still need to know why Mary was murdered in the first place? Anything further from Montreal regarding the mystery man, Pierre La Ville?"

"No, ma'am, not yet. I'll let you know as soon as I get any further information."

Susan felt a sense of frustration. It all seemed terribly like a waiting game. The Chief Inspector, Head of the Major Crimes Squad in London, was getting ready to shut down the investigation. They needed more information and soon.

· · ·

ROSE SPENT all morning cooking for the Memorial Service. There was nothing like food to bring people together. She made little baby quiches, sausage rolls, and several different dips to go with Nachos and veggies.

She cut three different cheeses and arranged them on a platter with grapes and crackers and then made up a batch of meat balls in a spicy tomato sauce.

She was just about to make several trays of assorted sandwiches when Tom came back from his game of golf.

"Can I do anything, love?"

Rose, who had worked non-stop since getting up that morning, was feeling suitably frazzled. She fairly snapped at him. "Well, you can make us some lunch, Tom."

Tom knew when to keep quiet. He got out some cold cuts and made a platter of sandwiches and put the kettle on for some tea.

"Would you like me to put some plastic wrap over these platters, love?"

Rose said, "Yes, and when you've done that you can start to load this stuff into the car for me. I'll have to get this down to the Town Hall soon. People will start to arrive way before 2.oopm."

"Is anyone going to do a eulogy?" Tom asked.

"I asked Graham and George Stokes if they would like to say a few words and I'm going to read out the prayer to St. Francis."

"Come on, love, stop what you're doing for a while and have some lunch." Tom insisted and Rose, for once, listened to her husband and joined him at the table.

"You said that this Pierre La Ville will be coming and that he wants to talk to you afterwards. How will you know who he is?"

"Well, by a process of elimination, Tom. I know pretty well everyone else so he should stand out as the stranger."

After lunch, Tom carried out the platters of food and Rose and he drove to the Town Hall and off loaded everything. They set up the food on a long table placed in the centre of the room. Rose had picked some beautiful white Hydrangeas from their garden and had arranged them in a large vase as a table centre piece.

By 1:00 p.m. there was a steady trickle of people and by 2:00 p.m. Rose counted forty. She breathed a sigh of relief as at the back of her mind she had wondered if anyone would show up at all.

The Croquet Club was well represented with at least twenty members and then the fitness class ladies made up the rest apart from the Stokes family, George, Graham, and even Jean had come.

Right at the back of the hall Rose saw Susan Parker and three of her officers in full uniform.

Rose looked around for Pierre La Ville. At first, she could see no stranger in the room. The service began, the eulogies spoken, then Rose read her prayer. Food was passed around and people quietly mingled.

Suddenly Rose was aware of a man standing by her side. He was, by the looks of things, in his late forties or possibly early fifties. A pleasant face, dark hair, smiling eyes, tall and well-groomed, and was wearing a jacket and tie. He put out his hand as he introduced himself.

"Hallo, I'm Pierre La Ville. You must be Rose Blair?"

"Yes, I'm Rose and my husband, Tom, is over there," Rose said pointing across the room to where Tom was deep in conversation with the president of the Croquet Club.

"Pierre, how long had you known Mary?"

"Let me think," Pierre said, "She came to Canada in 1995 so I have known her for over eighteen years."

"Well, I had only known her for one year and to be honest, I didn't even know very much about her personal life."

Pierre looked around the room and then spoke seriously. "There are many things that I'm not at liberty to tell you, Rose, but I can tell you this. Your friend was a very brave woman, and she suffered a tremendous loss in her life."

Rose interrupted Pierre saying, "Let me tell you what I think. I reckon that she lost her husband and children. Tell me if I'm correct?"

"Yes, you are, but how did you know? I'm sure that Mary would never have told you herself."

"Oh, Pierre, Mary never told anyone anything about herself. It's just that I saw a photograph by the side of her bed, and she claimed that it was her sister and family. I just put two and two together. Who exactly are you and how is it that you know so much about her?"

Pierre paused before he spoke gently.

"I am her case worker."

Rose looked astonished, "Case worker? You mean like a social worker?"

"Yes, I suppose a bit like that. I have been around mostly to make sure everything went smoothly for Mary."

"But why did she need a case worker?" Rose asked clearly perplexed by it all.

"That I cannot answer, but I did want to meet with you in person so that I could say thank you. Mary was the happiest that I have ever known her to be this past year living in Bayfield, and it's very largely due to you."

"Pierre, you said that Mary came to Canada in 1995. Where did she come from?"

Pierre La Ville was silent and then he shrugged his shoulders as if making up his mind.

"I shouldn't be telling you this, Rose, but I can trust that you won't spread this to anyone else. Mary came from Croatia. Her whole family was killed over there in 1992 and she came here to start a new life."

"Oh my gosh. Poor Mary. How absolutely terrible. But has this anything to do with her murder?"

"Yes, I'm afraid so. There have been at least three other people from Croatia like Mary who have either gone missing or have been murdered. We are seeing a connection, unfortunately."

"Well, I still don't understand what this is all about but at least I know a little more about my friend. Thank you for sharing some of this with me."

Pierre glanced over his shoulder to the door and then looked at his watch.

"Now, I really must go. Could you be so kind as to drop me a line when this case has been tied up? I'm on my way to Ilderton to the Croatian Centre just south of the town. Another one of my clients has gone missing and his family is distraught."

"And you still cannot tell me what it is you actually do? A case worker you say?"

Pierre was getting ready to leave. He took Rose's hand and said quietly,

"Rose, I work for the government. What I do has to be kept very quiet as my clients lives depend on it. It has been a pleasure meeting you."

Rose watched as Pierre La Ville left the room.

Susan Parker came up to her shortly afterwards. "Rose, who was that man you were talking to?"

"Oh, you wouldn't know him. His name is Pierre La Ville."

"What?" Susan shouted and started to run after Pierre. She returned a few minutes later. "I was too late. He had already pulled out in his car. What were you two talking about?"

Rose told Susan most of what Pierre had told her, but she omitted the part about Mary coming from Croatia.

"I was right about one thing, Susan. Mary did have a husband and children. They were all killed."

"So, Rose, let me get this straight. Pierre told you that he was a case worker and that he worked for the government?"

"Yes, he was heading over to Ilderton where he was going to check out another one of his clients.

Well, not exactly check him out because he's gone missing."

Rose could see that Susan was looking more and more confused.

"Oh, Susan, he just told me that several of his clients had either gone missing or have been murdered like Mary. That's all I know."

"Well, you have found out more in half an hour than we have in one week. I knew that this Pierre La Ville held the key to unlocking Mary's past. Thank you, Rose, you've been most helpful."

Rose wasn't sure how but at least she had established a couple of facts. Mary was from Croatia and she had been married with two children all of whom had been killed in 1992. She had come to Canada in 1995.

Croatia, now where exactly was Croatia, Rose thought. *I must check it out on the internet.*

That evening Rose went on the computer and Googled Croatia. According to Wikipedia, Croatia was part of what used to be known as Yugoslavia.

She called out to Tom. "Tom, can you remember when we back-packed all over Europe and we ended up in Yugoslavia? Remember how we fell in love with the country and you promised to take me back sometime? Well, did you know that Croatia, Serbia, and Bosnia are part of what was then Yugoslavia where Mary Stokes came from?"

Tom wandered over to where Rose was sitting in front of the computer scrolling down through a list of dates.

"Look, in 1991 there was a siege in Dubrovnik which lasted for seven months. Didn't we stay in that little hostel down by the old harbour in Dubrovnik? You know, that one that had no running water, only a well in the courtyard and the dormitories were strictly split between men and women.

Oh, but it was so pretty and old and I remember that courtyard with crimson red bougainvillea tumbling over the stone walls and the cobbled alleyways.

Remember how I twisted my ankle on those cobbles, and we had to stay on an extra few days so that I could rest up?"

Tom laughed. "Yes, and I also remember how we missed the ferry that was to take us to Venice, and we had to reschedule everything. It was like a deck of cards. Can you remember how difficult it was to change our flight from Milan?"

Rose sighed. Those were the days before air flight was so popular and Air Italia only flew twice a week to Toronto. But they had managed finally to get on a flight back home although it wouldn't have mattered if they had stayed another week apart from the fact that they would have run out of cash.

Neither Tom nor Rose had jobs to go back to. They had decided to wait until they got home before seriously looking for work.

In those days one had the luxury of being able to pick and choose where you wanted to work. Rose had told Tom that he should get a job first and then she would look for a teaching post afterwards and that is exactly what happened.

The summer of '72 would forever remain special to Tom and Rose. The summer of their carefree days of travelling throughout Europe, the days before mortgages and children and conforming to work schedules. The summer of love.

Rose was up past midnight on the computer. In the end, Tom, who had gone to bed at 10:30 p.m., had sleepily appeared and physically dragged her off to bed saying, "Enough, is enough, Rose. Bedtime."

ELEVEN

Over breakfast the following day Rose told Tom what she had discovered on the internet.

"Well, you know that we were reminiscing about the old Yugoslavia and the fact that Mary was Croatian. I looked up Croatia and boy, the history of that whole region is phenomenal. Look, I printed it all off. I'm going to read it all thoroughly today."

Tom looked at his wife incredulously and said, "But what exactly are you trying to prove, Rose?"

"Tom, the key to Mary's murder is tied up to her past, of that I am sure. I'm going through the political history of Croatia in the 90s, as that was the period which would have affected Mary. She came to Canada in 1995 so before that date something must have happened."

"Well best of luck, darling. It will be a bit like looking for a needle in a haystack. Now, what have you got on today other than researching the politics of Croatia? I'm off to play golf with Doug."

Rose glanced at the calendar and then gasped. "Oh my gosh, it's my book club today and I haven't even finished the book." With that she jumped up and hastily cleared away the breakfast dishes. She could get some reading in before the book club if she hurried.

. . .

SUSAN MANAGED to get 50 laps of the pool in before her team meeting. She always felt so invigorated after a swim, it cleared her head too.

"Good morning everyone. I'll make this meeting brief as I have to be in London by eleven this morning. I have to meet with the Chief. Now tell me some good news. This case is going stale on us."

Constable Mathieson stood up, a sheet of paper in his hands.

"I did a bit of research, ma'am, and cross-referenced Ljuba Strugar's name with other known Serbian criminals. It appears that he has been operating under the radar here in Canada but back in his old country it is a different story. His father, Pavle is currently serving time in Belgium for war crimes committed in the 90s. Ljuba escaped Serbia with his brother Milo and came to Canada in 1995. Both Ljuba and Milo are persons of interest on Interpol's list. That is all that I have to report at the moment, but I do have feelers out for them and I'm sure I'll get more information soon."

"Thank you, Constable. Well, I have some interesting information to share with you all. Our mysterious Pierre La Ville was here in Bayfield. He attended the memorial service for Mary Stokes and spoke to Rose Blair.

We now know a little more about Mary's past life. She apparently came to Canada in 1995 from Croatia, coincidently the same time as the Strugar brothers.

Her husband and two children were killed in 1992, another thing that Rose Blair was correct about. Pierre La Ville mentioned to Rose that some of his other clients had gone missing too. One had even been found murdered by a bolt from a crossbow. He was on his way to Ilderton where there is, apparently, a large Croatian community. One of his clients living there had gone missing. Sergeant, please can you look into the Croatian connection for us. The two are obviously linked somehow."

Sergeant Flowers stood up and said, "If Ljuba Strugar was a contracted assassin, surely whoever sent him on this mission, will be wanting to complete what was unfinished business. Should we not still be keeping the Blair home under surveillance, ma'am?"

"Good observation, Sergeant, and one that had crossed my mind too. We will keep up the surveillance but discreetly. I do not want to alarm the Blair's unnecessarily. Right, any more questions because if we have finished here, I need to be on the road."

The team gathered together and chatted amongst themselves while Susan collected her laptop and said her goodbyes.

The drive to London was uneventful. As Susan passed the cemetery, she glanced down the leafy entrance way and felt amazed that it had only been mere days since she had first arrived at the scene of the crime. It felt like months ago.

Instead of driving through Exeter, Susan decided to turn right at Airport Line just before getting to Brucefield. She kept going past the Hensall road, Dashwood Road, through Centralia and the Business Research Centre, finally turning left at Mount Carmel Road and back onto the highway.

She stopped at Lucan and picked up a Tim Horton's coffee, although she had seen an interesting café next to the Lucan Donnolly Museum when driving through the town. It was called The Stuffed Zucchini.

If Susan had more time, she would have stopped there for a bite to eat rather than at Timmy's, but time was of the essence.

She continued back on the road driving through the hamlets of Birr and Ava and then on down into London, crossing Fanshawe Park Road and on to Richmond Street.

Susan looked out over the city she called home and realized just how much she had missed it.

She loved living in the city, particularly London which was an easy city to navigate. If she had time after her meeting, she would pop over to her house in Wortley Village which was in the old south.

She had just that year bought her very first home, having always lived in apartments before. Her home was on Edward Street and it was a far cry from her Spring Bank Road condo.

But she loved her little house, an Ontario cottage style, two bedrooms, compact with a fantastic established and beautifully landscaped garden.

It had been one of those impulsive buys, probably one that she should never had contemplated, but so far, she had loved every minute of it and just adored Wortley Village itself.

Her neighbours' daughter had been looking after her two cats, Simba and Sara and she had a landscaping contractor coming in to cut the grass once a week.

The house was being looked after in her absence, but she still missed her home and was eager to visit it soon.

The Chief Inspector sat solidly behind his large, mahogany desk. He was an imposing figure of a man even sitting down. Thick, dark grey hair, a receding hairline, and a grey beard, he always wore a suit, shirt, and tie, immaculately ironed and very formal.

Looking up from his computer when Susan came in. He gruffly indicated that she take a seat.

Susan always felt like a naughty schoolgirl being sent to the Principal when she met with her boss.

"Right, I see from your report that the perpetrator has been contained, yet you say the motive for the murders are still unclear. How long do you think that it is going to take to tie this investigation up?"

Susan looked uncomfortable. "We are getting more information from Interpol as we speak. We have been hampered by government red tape, sir, which has severely slowed up our investigation. Our victim, it appears, was a foreign national from Croatia. The paid assassin, Ljuba Strugar appears to be from Serbia. There is a connection here that has eluded us so far, but I believe that we are getting closer to understanding the implications.

I am hopeful that within a week we should have some answers to our questions."

The Chief listened quietly and said nothing for a few minutes. Finally, he spoke slowly and deliberately.

"I'll give you four days to wrap it all up. Right, be back here with your final report in four day's time. Good day."

Susan had been dismissed. She left the office feeling somewhat slighted. She knew that it was just his manner to be gruff but surely a bit of pleasant talk would not be too hard to ask for?

She looked at her watch. The meeting had lasted all of ten minutes. She would have plenty of time to pop back home and have a visit with her cats.

I might even have time to call into the Black Walnut and pick up a sandwich, Susan thought as she drove into Wortley Village, up the main street, right at the supermarket, and right again onto Edward Street.

She could see her lovely little house in the distance. It was an old Ontario cottage quaint and pretty from the outside but totally impractical on the inside. The previous owners hadn't altered the cottage one single bit and as a result the interior was made up of small, dark rooms.

One day, Susan thought, she would make the whole inside open plan and let in the much needed light. Susan's heart quickened with delight as she approached her house. Oh, home sweet home.

ROSE ARRIVED at Becky's house with ten minutes to spare. Becky lived in Bayfield Meadows in a new house, just off Lidderdale, on Sweet Grass Lane.

Becky and her husband, David had retired to Bayfield from Waterloo and had purchased one of the first of the homes in the new, small subdivision known as Bayfield Meadows.

There were ten ladies in the book club, all newcomers to Bayfield, some newer than others.

Over the years they had all become best of friends and Rose really loved their comradeship and warm support.

Everyone was comfortable with each other, able to say what they thought, knowing that whatever was said at the book club stayed at the book club.

She greeted Becky warmly and sat down on a comfortable armchair. There were squares and cookies, cheese, crackers, and wine all laid out on the table. Coffee and tea were being passed around.

Linda, Julie, Carol, Leslie, Joanne, Helen, and Breda were all chatting away.

Rose looked over to where her friend Helen was sitting. Helen was a retired professor from Cambridge University; her subject specialty was European History.

I must ask her about Serbia and Croatia, Rose thought as she got up and put some caramel squares on a plate and sat back down on a chair next to Helen.

It always took the ladies ages to settle down to the business of discussing the book. Catching up with each other's news was the first call of the day.

"Hi, Helen, have you been having a good summer?" Rose asked. Helen had her grandchildren stay with her every summer for two or three weeks at a time.

By the end of the summer, she always looked ready for a holiday herself. Rose liked Helen. She was always an intelligent conversationalist, yet she had a wicked sense of humour.

"The first lot of grandchildren go home tomorrow. Andy and I then have three days to ourselves before the next load of little darlings arrive for two weeks. I'm exhausted just thinking about it."

Rose laughed. She knew what Helen felt like although this summer Tom and she had been let off quite lightly as Abby and Ella had only stayed a couple of weekends.

"Helen, I wonder if I could pop over later on today and pick your brains about the Serbian Croatian war in the early 90s?"

"Sure, Rose, I won't ask you why because knowing you there is some serious reason. How about coming around about 3:00 p.m. That will give me time to fish out some notes.

Becky called the ladies to order and their book discussion commenced.

On the way back to Bayfield, Susan decided to a make a small detour to Ilderton. She had not been there for a few years and was amazed at how the small village had mushroomed. New subdivisions had sprung up all along the road as far as the eye could see. Soon the village would be part of the London conurbation.

It was a shame, Susan thought as she drove past the pub, The Crown, and slowed down at the sign for the Croatian Centre. She was just pulling up to park the car when she spotted several police cruisers and a cordoned off area with the ubiquitous yellow tape flying about in the wind. Susan's heart sank.

This could mean only one thing. She got out of her car and walked purposely over to the police officers.

"What is going on here, men?" They looked startled.

Susan pulled out her badge saying unnecessarily, "I'm Inspector Parker from the Major Crimes Unit. Can someone please tell me what we have here?" She said pointing to the yellow taped area.

It was just then that Susan saw him. Pierre La Ville, standing with his head in his hands, obviously in great distress. Before the men could answer her question, Susan had walked over to Pierre and put her hand on his shoulder saying, "Pierre, I would like to have a word with you, please. I am Inspector Parker and I have been working the Mary Stokes murder inquiry."

He looked up and nodded saying, "They found him, you know, with a bolt through his chest, just like Mary. You know something, Inspector, this rests so heavily on my heart. It was my job to protect these people and I've failed my duty miserably."

Susan could feel his misery, but this was no time for emotions.

"Pierre, come with me back to my car. We need to talk. You have a lot of explaining to do."

Rose came back from the book club feeling happy and content with the world. Chatting with her friends, pouring out their worries, and offering and receiving words of advice always had a soothing effect on her soul. That was why Rose loved her group of book club ladies so much.

Tom returned from his game of golf in high spirits. Normally Doug beat him. His ranking was ten over par whereas Tom seemed to never get lower than twelve. But today, Tom had come out top with an eight over par and he was thrilled with himself.

Golf absolutely bored Rose but she recognized the fact that Tom loved the game and was happy that, combined with his love of sailing, he had been able to fill his retirement days with pleasurable pursuits. Life was too short, and one should be able to be a little hedonistic in retirement.

Rose did not want to eat any lunch as she had eaten too much at the book club, but she had some leak and potato soup in the fridge which she could heat up for Tom. There was also a wheel of ripe brie which he could have with some artisan bread and her peach chutney. With his lunch sorted Rose sat down opposite of Tom and chatted away.

"So, I'm going over to Helen's house this afternoon and she's going to give me a history lesson."

"Rose, you never stop, do you?" Tom said smiling. His wife was incorrigible but that was one of the reasons why he loved her.

At 3:00 p.m. Rose drove over across to Cameron Street where Helen lived. Andy, Helen's husband, sometimes went sailing with Tom. The two men got on well together and there had been some talk of the two couples sailing the boat across the lake to Michigan and making a weekend out of it.

Helen opened the front door. "Come on in, you just have to

excuse the mess. Andy and I haven't tidied up from the grandchildren yet."

Rose looked around and could see signs of children's activities all over the place. There was a half-finished jig-saw puzzle on the dining room table and Lego all over the floor.

An art easel and paints were set up by the window and various action men were lying on the sofa. You didn't have to be a detective to deduce that her grandchildren were both boys, very active little boys at that.

"Right, I'll put the kettle on first. What would you like? Tea or coffee?"

"Tea for me, please, Helen."

Rose sat on a wooden stool up against the kitchen island in Helen's kitchen. There was still the debris from their lunch left to be cleared away. Helen grabbed the plates and mugs and quickly loaded up the dishwasher.

"Sorry about the mess, Rose, you know me, housework is not my forte."

Rose laughed. That was what she liked about her friend, Helen. She was really down to earth.

"So, are you going to tell me what this is all about or is it a secret?"

Rose relayed what little that she knew about Mary Stokes ending up with the fact that she had discovered that Mary was Croatian.

"You see, Helen, I'm convinced that her past is the key to why she was murdered."

"Well, my friend, the Serbian /Croatian war does tie in with the dates you've mentioned. Somehow Mary was involved either actively or politically.

Let me give you a brief history of that region. One of the first things you must know about the period you are interested in is that after the breakup of Yugoslavia in 1991 the Serb-Montenegrin forces lay siege to Dubrovnik and this lasted seven months. Was Mary from Dubrovnik?"

Rose replied hesitantly. "I'm not sure, but Tom and I spent some time in the old harbour there. We stayed in a very rustic, but beautiful old hostel back in the 70's."

"Well, that whole area was known as Dalmatia. Its history is both colourful and varied dating back to the 7th century. The city itself was part of the Byzantine Empire and then, after the crusades in the 12th century, it came under the sovereignty of Venice. Between the 14th and 18th century the area ruled itself as a free state although it still had to pay an annual tribute to the Sultan of the Ottoman Empire. By the 15th century Portuguese refugees had flooded the city. Then, in 1667 a catastrophic earthquake killed over 5,000 people. In 1806 Dubrovnik surrendered to the Napoleonic army. However, in 1814 it was recaptured by the British-Austrian troops under Captain Sir William Hoste.

According to the Congress of Vienna, in 1815 Croatia came under the Habsburg Empire."

Helen stopped her lecture and proceeded to pour them both out a cup of tea. She continued her monologue ignoring the glazed look in her friend's eyes.

"In 1918, after the fall of the Austria–Hungary alliance at the onset of the Great War, the Kingdom of Yugoslavia was created, made up of Serbs, Croats, and Slovenes. During the Second World War, Dubrovnik became part of the Nazi-puppet state of Croatia. In October 1944, President Tito's troops entered Dubrovnik and it became part of communist Yugoslavia. More than 80 influential and well-known citizens, including priests, were executed without trial on the island of Daksa. The Communist regime continued to persecute the Croats."

Helen paused briefly before continuing.

"In 1991, Croatia and Slovenia declared their Independence from Yugoslavia. The Yugoslav People's Army attacked the Croatian Military. The regime in Montenegro, led by Momir Bulatovic, joined forces even though in Dubrovnik only six percent of the population were actually Serbs. On October 1, 1991, Dubrovnik was attacked by the Yugoslav People's Army under the leadership of Serbian President Milosevic. A siege was laid that would last for seven months. Many civilians were killed and wounded. Of the buildings in the city, 56 percent were badly damaged, some of them UNESCO World Heritage sites. The old city wall sustained 650 hits by artillery rounds."

Once again Helen paused, but this time she appeared to be deep in thought. She turned to Rose and spoke softly to her friend. "You know something, Rose. I reckon that your friend Mary must have been somehow involved in this siege. You said that her whole family was killed. Well, many civilians died during this attack. Look, it says here," Helen pointed to a paragraph on the typed sheet of paper she held, "General Pavle Strugar was sentenced to prison by the International Criminal Tribunal Court in The Hague. They are still holding trials for war crimes committed years ago in Bosnia, Serbia, and Croatia. That President Milosovic had been indicted for ethnic cleansing of the most diabolical nature. Mass genocides and brutal executions. Truly horrific. Just maybe Mary was witness to some of this. Look, take this home with you and read through it all again. I'm sorry that I've had to condense it all like this."

"Thank you so much, Helen. There is so much to digest. What a history."

Rose left soon afterwards feeling quite overcome by her history lesson.

She drove back to Bayfield Terrace in a daze but as she approached her house her fog lifted. She simply adored her home as it was always so welcoming, and she couldn't wait to be inside chatting away to Tom who without fail had a calming influence on her when she had a troubled soul.

TWELVE

Susan swam up and down, up and down, first doing an invigorating crawl and then a gentler breaststroke. After thirty laps she got out of the pool, towel dried her body, and then went back to her room. She would still have time to make a quick call to Henri before her team meeting at 9:00am.

She tapped in his number.

"Oh, *ma cheri, Je t'adore, Comment ca va?*"

"Oh Henri, English please. Now I need some help. I'm afraid that there has been another murder down here in a small town called Ilderton, just north of London. The murder was almost identical to that of Mary Stokes, a crossbow bolt through the victim's chest. You know Ljuba Strugar from the Serbian syndicate, the man we caught in Bayfield? Apparently, he has a brother named Milo. We believe that the perpetrator of this latest murder is this man Milo. Could you alert your team in Montreal? This man is armed and dangerous. He needs to be apprehended before we have another murder on our hands."

Susan finished her conversation with Henri and then prepared to leave for The Lion's Hall. Five minutes later she pulled up in front of building and jumped out of her car.

"Good morning, everyone. We have much work to do. Yesterday, I met with Pierre La Ville, yes, our mystery man himself. He has managed to fill in many of our blanks regarding Mary Stokes. He was her case worker. She was part of a Witness Protection plan. Her real name is Maria Krupl, formerly of Dubrovnik, Croatia. Maria gave evidence at the International Criminals Tribunal at The Hague in Belgium and was put in the Witness Protection Program afterwards. She came to Canada in 1995 and had been under Pierre La Ville's watch ever since then. Now here's the thing, another murder took place just yesterday outside of Ilderton. The victim, Ian Ross, was also in the same Witness Protection Program as another of Pierre La Ville's clients."

Susan opened her notebook and continued to read from it.

"There has, apparently, been four similar cases, two murders and two disappearances of his clients. Pierre is devastated. They all gave evidence in the War Crimes Court and all were Croatian. Now we do know that Ljuba Strugar was one of the killers, but I suspect that his brother, Milo, has been in on this vendetta too probably working as a team with his brother. I have already called Inspector Le Bruin in Montreal to alert the police in Quebec, but if my suspicions are correct our man is somewhere much closer than Quebec. We need to find this man fast before another victim is murdered. Montreal will be sending through a photograph of Milo Strugar soon."

Sergeant Flowers got up to speak, "So, ma'am, what exactly is their motive for murdering all of these people in the Witness Protection Program?"

"Good question, Sergeant. It appears that Ljuba and Milo's father was General Pavle Strugar. All of the murdered victims gave evidence at the International Criminal Tribunal in 1995 against him and as a consequence he was sentenced to a hefty prison sentence. We're not sure but it appears possible that these killings are in retaliation for the condemning evidence given, a vendetta of sorts. The Serbian gang leaders have a mob mentality, an eye for an eye, a tooth for a tooth, not much different from any other organized crime syndicates. Just look at the Italian and Russian mafia."

Susan paused as she gathered up her papers and then continued, "Anyway, Team, we need to find this man and quickly. Constable Mathieson, Constable Elliot and Brown, show this photograph around. Go to Exeter, Seaforth, Clinton, Goderich, and of course Bayfield. Sergeant Flowers, I need you to liaise with Inspector Le Bruin and his team in Montreal. Keep all the channels open. We need to crack this case open now."

Susan wrapped up the meeting and sighed deeply. She hoped that they would succeed in tracking down Milo Strugar but she couldn't help thinking of the previous year's fiasco with Jim Reynolds and how he had completely slipped through their net.

TOM HAD COME HOME the previous day with a present for Rose. When she opened the small box, she found a cell phone, a Samsung smart phone, nestled in some tissue paper.

He had kissed her and said that he wanted her to carry it with her at all times and to make sure that she kept the power on. Rose had thanked Tom but secretly had thought that it was a waste of money. She would, however, show willing and put it in her purse.

The day had started gently. Both Tom and Rose had gotten up leisurely and had a lazy breakfast.

Tom was going out to play golf but not until eleven and Rose should have been going to her fitness class but had decided to give it a miss that day because she just wanted to enjoy the morning without any obligations.

Puff and Ben also appeared reluctant to get up and start the day.

Even after Rose and Tom had got dressed and were sitting eating their breakfast, both dogs still lay fast asleep in their beds.

"I think that I'll take those lazy dogs for a walk later on." Rose said as she cleared away their breakfast. "I haven't taken them down to the beach in a while. Yes, that's what I'll do after I've done a bit of housework. What time will you be back, my love?"

Tom was engrossed in his paper and he hadn't heard a word of what Rose had said.

Rose coughed loudly.

"I said, what time will you be back from your game of golf?" Rose repeated with a slight edge to her voice.

"Oh, umm... golf, not before about 2:00 p.m. We'll probably grab a bite to eat at the club house so don't save any lunch for me."

"Righty-ho then," Rose said, "I'll just zip around with the vacuum cleaner and then I'll take the dogs for a walk."

Eleven o'clock came around and Tom collected his golf bag and went off with Doug for a round of golf at The Maitland Golf course in Goderich."

Rose grabbed the two leashes and her purse, called Puff and Ben, clipped on their leashes, and off they went heading for Pioneer Park.

It was another beautiful August morning. Already the temperature was up in the 80's. It was going to be a scorching hot day. They reached Pioneer Park and Rose looked around. Nobody was about so she knelt down to unleash the dogs.

Just as she bent down, Puff let out a growl. Rose felt the air whoosh past her before she saw the arrow which narrowly missed her head.

Rose screamed and ran for the steps leading down to the beach. Turning around she saw a man crouching on one knee while reloading another bolt into his crossbow.

She ran for her life. Puff and Ben barked but then took off in pursuit of Rose. Fortunately, some people were just coming up the steps as Rose was running down.

She shouted to them, "He tried to kill me", and pointed up

towards the clump of trees by the fence where she had seen the man holding his crossbow in his hand.

Rose remembered her new cell phone. She grabbed her purse and dialed in 911.

"Please come quickly, Pioneer Park, Bayfield, a man tried to kill me!"

Fortunately, Tom had loaded some essential numbers on the phone under the favourites on her contact list. Rose was able to call Susan who said, "Stay low, a car will be on its way soon."

Rose answered, "Fortunately I've got some people here with me, but it looks as if the man has run away. I heard a car head off south down Tuyll Street at high speed."

"Did you manage to get a good look at him, Rose?"

Rose thought for a minute. Everything had happened so quickly.

She closed her eyes and tried to visualize the man she had seen by the trees. He was crouched down so it was difficult to ascertain his height.

"Susan, he was very dark, with black curly hair, clean shaven, definitely looked Eastern European or possibly Asian. He had a biggish nose, oh, and he wore a long-sleeved yellow shirt and I think, blue pants, that's about all that I can remember."

"Well, that was great, Rose. A police car has been dispatched to Tuyll Street and another to Pioneer Park. Hold on, we'll be there soon."

"But Susan, seriously, I don't need any help now, but you do need to go after that man. He's probably on Cameron Street by now, you need to head over in that direction and try to intercept him there."

"Alright, Rose, but I still want you to stay put until someone gets there. Have you contacted Tom? I don't want you left on your own."

At the mention of Tom's name Rose gulped. He hadn't yet been told but why worry him, she thought.

I'm fine and the dogs are restless, I'll just go back home and make myself a cup of tea.

It was strange, Rose thought, the last time when that man had broken into their house and she had hidden in the closet, she had felt absolutely terrified, but this time, all she felt was surreal. Had she really almost been killed by a crossbow? It all felt like a dream, a weird dream, but definitely not real.

Rose walked slowly back along Bayfield Terrace until she came to the Mara Street turning. *The dogs had been deprived of their walk on the beach, the danger was over*, Rose thought. She would still take them for a run on the sand.

She loved going down the little dirt track called Mara Street that led to the Marina and peer. It was like walking through an enchanted forest with wildflowers growing everywhere and the trees bent over like a tunnel shutting out the sunlight while at the same time creating a magical, leafy throughway.

Rose had to watch how she walked as it was quite a steep foot path and the dogs tended to pull rather at their leashes. She almost slid down the last part of the walk and then the trees opened out to the paved road and the Marina with all its big, power boats.

Rose looked across to where Tom had his boat docked. She could see the pretty boat gently bobbing up and down on the water. She looked up to the bluff of Harbour Lights and without fail she could visualize Captain Bayfield envisioning a military fort built on the cliff looking out over the water.

But what a great strategic position to build such a fort it would have been. Of course, it never happened. The Royal Military, British of course, ran out of money and no forts were ever built on the shores of Lake Huron.

Baron Van Tuyll had bought thousands of acres of land, in fact the whole of Bayfield, on the assumption that the Royal Military would purchase the land off him for a premium price.

This never happened and he was forced to sell the bulk of the land off at a low price to Malcom Cameron just so that he could settle his taxes.

Rose was brought back to the present day by Ben and Puff tugging at their leads. They could smell the water. Rose got to the beach and looked around. There was nobody on the sand or in the water, the dogs were in luck.

She unleashed then and they charged off heading straight for the lake.

Ben splashed his way into the water and immediately started to swim looking very much from a distance like an otter.

Puff, on the other hand, would not go in the water until Rose had thrown him a stick and then he happily obliged by fetching it and having a good swim at the same time.

Rose was so engrossed in the game of fetch the stick that she neither saw nor heard the silver car pull into the car park. A dark headed, swarthy complexioned man got out of the car and reached inside for something.

It was at that moment that Puff stopped in mid-air, dropped the stick that was in his mouth, and started to bark so loudly that Rose was alarmed.

Puff started to run towards the man by the car. Rose looked on with horror as he aimed his crossbow at her beloved dog. Ben, who had been silently watching the whole proceeding, growled a low, menacing snarl. He charged like a bullet towards the man knocking Puff over just as the bolt from the crossbow was released.

Rose screamed, "No," thinking that Puff had been hit. She grabbed the nearest thing that she could find. A long piece of drift-wood, and ran towards the man and her dogs.

Ben was upon him, snarling and biting at his ankles and Puff, recovered, joined in snapping and nipping at his legs.

"Get your bloody dogs off me." He yelled with a thick accent.

Rose lifted the piece of driftwood that she was carrying and, raising it above her head, she struck the man's hand which was holding the crossbow.

The weapon ended up in the sand in front of Rose. She grabbed it and then thought, *Now what am I meant to do? I've never shot one of these in my life. I haven't a clue what to do with it.*

The man struggled to break free from the dogs. Kicking out at them made them attack him with even greater frenzy. Rose was undecided what to do and then she remembered her cell phone. Still holding the deadly crossbow, she tapped in Susan's number. It was picked up straight away.

"Susan, Susan, please come quickly. I'm on the beach by the pier and I've got your man. But please hurry."

Ben let out a yelp as the man kicked him viciously. Puff went to the rescue and sunk his teeth into the bare flesh of the man's leg. He screamed, "Get these dogs off me!"

Rose stood by and continued to watch the dogs circling him and charging forth, lips curled, teeth bared.

Who would have thought that they could ever be so ferocious? *They're even scaring me,* Rose thought.

Suddenly the sound of police sirens could be heard getting louder and louder and then four officers came running towards Rose. When they had drawn their weapons Rose commanded the dogs to stop.

"Good dogs, sit." And the two dogs obediently pulled away from the man, tails wagging, and sat at Rose's feet.

"Boy, that was impressive," Susan said as she approached the man and roughly pushed his arms behind his back and cuffed him.

"Those brutes, evil animals, curs..." The man shouted as he was led away by Sergeant Flowers and Constable Elliot.

MUCH LATER, Rose lay in Tom's arms and kissed him.

"That's for buying me that smart phone. I reckon it saved my life."

Tom kissed her and then sat bolt upright in bed saying. "Oh, darling, I forgot to tell you, a package was couriered to you while you were out. With everything else going on I completely forgot about it."

Rose looked intrigued.

Tom got out of bed and disappeared into the living room returning shortly with a small package. He handed it over to Rose who opened it quickly.

Inside the packaging lay a small leather-bound journal. Rose opened it having already guessed the owner. She read the first few lines and her eyes welled up with tears.

"Oh my gosh, Tom. This is Mary's journal, and her real name is Maria Krupl. Look, there's a note from some solicitor, Messrs Anderson and Hays. They have forwarded this to me at Mary's instructions, as she had requested that it be sent to me in the event of her death. Oh Tom, this scares me. Mary must have suspected that she might be killed."

Maria's Journal
November 6th, 1991
Above all things be true to yourself. My mother used to say that to me when I was a gawky teenager growing up in the old city of Dubrovnik. To my mum, if she was alive, I would say that I am being true to myself when I admit that I am terrified. I am scared senseless. There, I said it. The past week has been nothing more than a night-mare and I really don't know where to begin. "Always begin at the beginning," Madam Orefors used to say. She was our English teacher at St. Blaise's Catholic School for Girls. But where is the beginning? Do I start with the political unrest leading up to 1991 and even then, when did that first start? I suppose an historian would pinpoint the beginnings of our troubles with the Austrian-Habsberg creation of the Kingdom of Dalmatia. The Croatian People's party and the Serbian Catholic parties were formed. These two parties divided the country and ultimately lead to the destruction of Yugoslavia. The Socialist Republic of Croatia was renamed the Republic of Croatia.

Just two weeks ago the JNA (Yugoslav People's Army) attacked the military in our city. I will always remember that awful day. My family and I watched dreadful war images on the television. Troops throwing tear gas, civilians being gunned down on the streets. None of us could believe what was happening in our beautiful city. Today the electricity went off. We have been told that it will come on for two hours a day. The city is, apparently under siege. Darko says that we need to begin to stockpile our food. Goran and Danica, our children, think that it is cool, us using candles. But it is getting cold and we have no heat. We are all wearing layers and layers of clothing to keep ourselves warm. Our radio gives us contact with the outside world and to this we are eternally grateful.

NOVEMBER 28TH, 1991

We managed to stockpile a whole box of 24 cans of tuna fish, dried milk, and canned tomatoes. The radio news announced that 19 citizens had been blown up by a missile. It has been unsafe for Goran and Danica to leave our house to go to school. They think that this is great news. On the radio we heard that Croatia had offered peace talks, but the offer had been rejected by the President of Serbia, Slobidan Milosevic. We also heard that 7,000 people have been evacuated by sea. Darko and I talked seriously about the necessity of us leaving the city, but we decided to stay.

DECEMBER 3RD, 1991

Humanitarian aid has started to arrive. A fleet of civilian boats sailed into the harbour bringing fresh food and provisions. The boats have offered to evacuate more refugees. Darko and I once again wondered if we should at least send out the children. But again, we resisted. To our horror the JNA resumed their mortar attacks on the city, mostly in our area of the old city. The radio told us that the bombardment was concentrated on the Stradun, the beautiful central promenade in town. 13 civilians were killed.

December 6th, 1991
Our university library has been destroyed along with over 20,000 books. The Libertas Hotel was also bombed and a ship, the Sveti Vlaho, was sunk by a wire guided missile. Still only short bursts of electricity. Gas bottles are in short supply. We have started to run out of canned tuna. Very little fresh produce for sale in the market. Darko says that the siege will be over before Christmas.

JANUARY 8TH, 1992

Just when we thought that the gunfire would never stop a cease fire was declared According to the radio the Sarajevo Agreement was signed by Croatia, the JNA and the United Nations. Darko was right. The siege is over. We all hope and pray that our lives will get back to normal soon.

FEBRUARY 8TH, 1992

The cease fire is no longer. Our lovely Hotel Grand was destroyed. Darko and I celebrated our anniversary there and now it has been completely bombed and burnt to the ground. Still very little food and no fresh produce.

MARCH 20TH, 1992

Today my life changed forever. I cannot write about it. My heart has been broken into a million little pieces. Darko, Goran, and Danica have been taken from me. My life is over.

March 25th, 1992
I have been in hiding for five days. In case I don't make it, let this be a record of what took place. I must write down the nightmarish

event before the details diminish in my mind. I have to bear witness to the atrocities of General Strugar. My account must be accurate because my voice will be heard.

The day my whole world was destroyed, just five days ago, began like any other day. Danika and Goran had resumed their schooling all but with shortened hours. Darko and I were back at work. My job as a medical secretary took me a little north of the city centre whereas Darko worked at the Bank of Croatia right downtown. That morning I waved goodbye to Danica and Goran, then Darko and I walked together until he reached the bank and then I cycled the next 3 kilometres to my work. All buses and public transport had been closed for months. There was no gas for cars, so the roads were pretty clear of vehicles other than the military trucks and jeeps, a frequent sight in the city.

I was cycling home when in the distance just outside Zjacobs chicken farm I saw two, huge black military trucks and a group of JNA soldiers just loitering outside with their machine guns hanging loosely in their hands. I got off my bicycle and tentatively walked in the shadows of the trees so that I could not be easily detected. Whenever there were soldiers hanging around, we all felt incredibly frightened and vulnerable. Suddenly the back of one of the trucks was thrown open and about twenty civilians, men, women, and children, came tumbling out. I watched mesmerized and then, to my horror, I saw them, my beloved family, Darko, Goran, and Danika, along with several other people that I recognized. They were being pushed into a line and made to follow the soldier in charge. I propped my bicycle up against a tree and stealthily followed the line of civilians and my own family. A soldier drew up the rear of the line and, with the butt of his machine gun prodded the civilians urging them to move on. The straggly line of men, women, and children turned into the farmyard. I hid behind one of the barns and then heard the soldier call out, "Strugar, the trench is ready." I find it difficult to write what happened next. It shook me to the core. But I must bear witness. The civilians and my darlings were lined up in front of the trench which looked like a deep ditch. Four soldiers stood behind the people who now had been told to put their hands-on top of their heads. Goran and Danica were crying but trying so hard to be brave. Darko, my darling husband looked to be talking, presumably trying to sooth our babies. The General suddenly gave the order to shoot and the four soldiers let fire with their machine guns. It was all over in ten seconds. I could not move. I was frozen with horror at what I had just witnessed. I could not avert my eyes from the nightmarish scene before me. It was like Dante's Inferno, only worse, just a mere 20 metres from where I had stood hidden behind the barn. The General then barked out another order and the soldiers started to drag the mutilated bodies and threw them in the trench. A back-hoe roared to life somewhere behind me.

Suddenly, a soldier shouted, and, to my horror, I saw him coming towards me. The next thing I knew I was running, running for my life. I got out into the lane and ran towards where I had left my bicycle. Grabbing it I peddled for all my worth in the opposite direction that the soldiers were running. I heard one of them shout out, "I know her, its Maria Krupl. She works at the Medical centre." And with that my fate was sealed.

APRIL 5TH, 1992

For two weeks I have been hiding. I didn't go back to our house for three days. I stayed with my friend Jazmine and then I decided what I would do. Firstly, I needed to go back to our home and find my passport, birth certificate, and pack some basic essentials in a small suitcase. I was convinced that the military would be looking for me so my friend Jazmine coloured my dark brown hair blond and cut it really short. A boat, I had been reliably told, would be leaving the harbour that next day and it would take me to Venice. My plan was to get myself to Belgium where I had an aunt and an uncle. They would protect me I was sure. The third part of my plan would be the most *difficult. I wanted to bear witness to the atrocities of General Strugars genocide. To do this I had to get to The Hague, to the Criminal War Tribunals Courts. I knew that I would never return to my beloved city. But I had to seek retribution for my family.*

APRIL 8TH, 1992

I succeeded in creeping into our house. I found all the paperwork that I needed and my passport, packed a suitcase with clothes, and finally, I grabbed a photograph taken on the steps of St. Blaise Cathedral in Dubrovnik. It showed Darko and me smiling into the camera. Darko had his arm over my shoulder and he looked so handsome that I let out a sob. My darling Goran and Danica stood in front of us both big smiles upon their faces. Danica's grin showed the gap in her front teeth and Goran, who had just lost one of his front teeth, looked like a little imp. What the camera didn't show was Danica pinching her little brother and Goran turning to pinch her back. I had just told them to stand still and smile. Tears rolled down my cheeks as I stuffed the precious photograph into my bag of papers.

I managed to board the boat quite easily. Nobody wanted to see any official papers. I kept my head down low every time I saw a soldier. We reached Venice ten hours later. I had very little money, but I knew that I had enough to buy a train ticket to Bruges in Belgium. My dear friend Jazmine had pressed one hundred euros into my hand as I departed. "God go with you, my friend," she had whispered as I left her tiny apartment.

APRIL 14TH, 1992

I have finally arrived at my Aunt Zib and Uncle Drago's house. Both my parents were dead. My mother was Aunt Zib's sister and there is a strong family resemblance. When I told them my story my aunt wept and said that I could stay with them for as long as I needed.

I then told them my plan to seek legal help from the Criminal Tribunal Courts of The Hague. My aunt and uncle promised to help.

ONE YEAR LATER....

January 8th, 1993

Finally, the United Nations Security Council Resolution have indicted Milosevic, Strugar, JoKic, and other commanding officers of the JNA. The International Criminal Tribunal for the former Yugoslavia trial began today. Who knows just how long the courts will take before justice prevails? I have met with the prosecution lawyers, told my story and offered to stand witness against these monsters. I have been advised to stay in hiding. The JNA have hit men trying to intimidate and eliminate any witnesses.

MARCH 20TH, 1993

Today, one year ago, I lost all my loved ones. My heart is still broken. Will it ever mend?

JUNE 10TH, 1993

I met today with a Canadian called Pierre La Ville. He has been assigned as my Case Worker. A few weeks ago, I had requested asylum in Canada. It seemed far enough away from Europe. I would be safe across the Atlantic. I was told that I would be put in a Witness Protection Program. This Pierre La Ville seems a kind enough man. I feel that I can trust him with my life.

JUNE 9TH, 1993

I attended as a witness to give testimony at the trial today. General

Strugar looked me in the eyes defiantly. I could have punched his eyes out. I was on the stand for all of five minutes for as long as it took for me to say my name and my address. I could see that the trial was going to be very protracted. Today, on television, I felt sick when they showed dreadful pictures of Sarajevo under the most dreadful artillery bombardment. Sniper shots could be heard as the journalist shouted over the noise of the guns. It hardly seems possible that just over two years ago I was living that nightmare myself in Dubrovnik.

AUGUST 13TH, 1993

I got to take the witness stand today and actually was given time to tell my story. My aunt and uncle were there to give me support and Pierre La Ville also turned up. Afterwards, we all went out to lunch. Pierre had some papers that he wanted me to sign. He then told me that my immigration papers had almost been processed. I could possibly be in Canada by the end of the year.

OCTOBER 9TH, 1993

My English is coming on well. I have also picked up quite a lot of French and Flemish too. Languages have always been my forte. My aunt owns a dress shop and I have been working for her since my escape from Dubrovnik.

Still, we see harrowing images on television of war-torn Sarajevo. Why has no one come to help the people of Sarajevo? I remember the Sarajevo Olympics in 1984. It was spectacular. Darko and I had only been married one year and we were so proud then as people of all nationalities had marvelled at the beauty of our country. Where are those people now?

November 12th, 1993

I am still waiting for news on my immigration. I am ready to start *my new life in the new world. I just want it to happen soon. Will this war never end?*

JANUARY 6TH, 1994

Pierre called today. He has all the necessary documents. I had to literally sign my life away. Well, my old life. I am to be called Mary. Mary Watson. I like my new name. Pierre has even arranged where I will live and work. I must now really practice my spoken English as Pierre says that it is important that I don't stand out. I must lose my accent.

MARCH 20TH, 1994

Two years since my life was turned upside down. My heart is still broken but I know now that I will survive. My English is pretty good even if I say so myself. The months of practice have paid off. Pierre has booked my flight. I leave in two months.

MAY 31ST, 1994

As I stood in the departures lounge of Brussels airport, I realized that I would no longer be able to say that I was European, let alone that I am Croatian. I had a tearful farewell from my aunt and uncle. They have been so kind to me. I owe them so much. I promised to write although Pierre had advised against me having any communication with any one from Europe. My flight was uneventful. I arrived at Toronto Pearson Airport early evening after a seven-hour flight. Pierre La Ville was there to meet me. My new life has begun.

DECEMBER 25TH, 1994

I celebrated Christmas, my first Christmas in Canada, with my neighbours in the apartment block where I live. Guelph is a pleasant enough city with a small town feel to it. There is a large Catholic church downtown and Sleeman's brewery on the outskirts. There is a river that runs through the centre and a beautiful park. It is a university city and I like that I will be amongst young people. I am beginning to feel at home. Nobody has guessed that I am not Canadian.

ONE YEAR LATER......

September 1995

I am working as a secretary at St. Vincent's Catholic Elementary school surrounded by young people. I often look at the students and I think to myself that Goran and Danica would be like them had they lived. Goran would have been ten and Danica, eight. I always look at the grades three and five students more than any other grades. I try to visualize my darlings and what they would look like now that they would have been four years older.

The janitor at the school is very friendly. His name is Graham Stokes. He has asked me out to The Bookshelf Café in downtown Guelph for lunch this Saturday.

October 31st, 1995

My first Halloween. Graham and I dressed up and went to Mike and Kim's Halloween Party. It was great. Graham is divorced and he has a boy, George, who is 15. Jean, Graham's ex drops George off every other weekend at his house. I have yet to meet him.

DECEMBER 15TH, 1995

Graham took me out to dinner last night and I went back to his house afterwards. It is the first time that I've slept with another man since Darko. I will always love Darko, but I definitely feel something for Graham.

. . .

DECEMBER 24TH, 1995

George is to spend Christmas with his father. I met him for the first time today. He is a moody, gawky teenager and he looks so much like Graham. I also briefly met his ex-wife Jean. She seemed very pleasant.

The war has finally ended in Sarajevo. An estimated 250,000 people have been killed over a period of three years. My heart goes out to each and every one of those families who have lost their loved ones in this horrific war.

FEBRUARY 25TH, 1996

Graham asked if I would marry him today and I said yes. He knows nothing about my past. I am not allowed to tell anyone.

March 20th, 1996

It is four years ago today that my life changed forever. Forgive me my darlings, for being alive and about to marry a man whom I'll never love as much as you.

APRIL 27TH, 1996

Graham and I had a quiet registry office wedding at Guelph Civic Hall. Afterwards we went out for lunch at The Bookshelf Café and then back home where we consumed a bottle of Champagne together.

SEPTEMBER 19, 1996

Started a new school year. Graham and I have settled into his house together very nicely. George comes to visit once or twice a month and he is coming out of his shell and talking to me more and more. I have noticed that Graham drinks way too much.

. . .

DECEMBER 4TH, 1996

Graham and I had our first argument today. I felt really threatened. He had been drinking steadily all evening and when I tried to take the bottle of Rye away from him, he turned nasty. George has been sent to the Bluewater Correctional Centre for drug offences.

FIVE YEARS LATER.......

April 27th, 2001

I have been married for 5 years now and am beginning to regret my decision to marry Graham Stokes. He continues to drink heavily and gets more and more aggressive every time he is drunk. Pierre La Ville says that I should leave him before he truly does me some harm. I don't know if I have the strength to leave.

OCTOBER 21ST, 2001

General Strugar has been transferred to the International Criminal Tribunal for the former Yugoslavia Prosecution courts. It has taken 7 years for the trial to get to this stage.

Graham has been attending AA. He took me away for the weekend to a lovely village on Lake Huron called Bayfield. We stayed at The Little Inn and it was like old times. We walked along the beach together and had lunch at The Albion. We even went into the quaint little library and met a delightful librarian called Angela. She suggested that we look around the Historical Societies Archives and we met a lovely lady called Lena. What a friendly village. I loved it.

MARCH 21ST, 2002

It is ten years since I lost my beloved family. Things have not been going great between Graham and me. He is back drinking again. George no longer visits. I have taken to sending him a $20 note every now and then. Graham has no time for his son. He calls him a loser and a druggy. Pierre still says that I should leave Graham.

One year later...
April 27th, 2003
I have been married to Graham for seven years today. His drinking problem is getting worse. I've begged him to go back to AA, but he refuses.

General Kovacevic was arrested today in Serbia and he has been transferred to the International Criminal Tribunal courts and charged with murder, cruel treatment, and violations of laws of war. These trials drag on and on.

THREE YEARS LATER...
March 11th, 2006
Slobodan Milosevic's trial was never completed. The evil man died while still in the ICTY custody. Kovacevic pleaded an insanity defence and the proceedings have been transferred to the courts in Serbia.

Graham and I are getting a divorce. I have moved out and now live in a small apartment right downtown very close to the Catholic Church. Still no news on a verdict for General Strugar. It has now been 12 years since I stood at the witness stand and told my story.

Two years later....
May 20th, 2008
General Strugar's trial and appeals process has been completed. The final verdict of conviction of crimes included attacks on civilians, violation of the laws of war, devastation not in keeping with the military, but no mention of genocide. His sentence was a mere seven years

in prison. When I heard this travesty of justice I broke down and cried. I contacted Pierre La Ville and demanded an explanation. He told me that he would look into it. When I think of the atrocities that man rendered and for that he just got a seven-year sentence. What about all those people murdered by this monster? I am so angry and upset I don't know what to do.

TWO YEARS LATER....

June 30th, 2010

I drove down to Bayfield from Guelph. I'm booked into the Deer Park for four days. Pierre is joining me at the weekend. We have got to know each other more intimately than I ever dared to think we would. I know that he is married, and I also know how unprofessional this all is, a case worker having an affair with his client, but no one will ever know. He helped me through a very vulnerable time when I was at my lowest ebb. The shock of hearing that General Strugar had been sentenced so lightly just pulled me over the edge of reason. All that I had lost and my whole life that had been compromised for such a lean sentence. It was just a like a slap in my face. Pierre had helped me get over my anger and sadness and we had fallen in love through the process. He is a gentleman and has brought me a sense of peace and calmness, something that I have not experienced for many years.

TWO YEARS LATER....

May 30th, 2012

I have finally done it. The last legal document has been signed. The cottage is officially mine. Bayfield is now my new home.

JUNE 6TH, 2012

I joined the Fitness Class today and met a lovely woman called

Rose Blair. She invited me back to her house for coffee and we spent two glorious hours just getting to know each other. Rose lives in an adorable house on Bayfield Terrace. It has a white picket fence and beautiful climbing rose bushes framing the front porch. Her husband, Tom, spends most of the summer sailing or playing golf. I feel so happy and blessed to have met Rose.

JULY 8TH, 2012

Today I met a lovely man called Michael. He is the grounds keeper at the cemetery. I've taken to going there and tending to the children's graves. Because I haven't been able to bury my own children, I feel that it is my duty to tend to all those other children who have had their precious lives cut short prematurely.

August 2nd, 2012

Michael and I have fallen in love. I have gone back to his trailer and made love for the first time since I left Graham. He is a kind and sensitive man.

SEPTEMBER 8TH, 2012

Rose and I have become best of friends. Today she convinced me to buy a bicycle from Outside Projects. It was lovely cycling around the village together. Tom invited me to go on a sunset sail with Rose and him. Their boat is gorgeous. Rose made some croissants filled with salmon, some little phyllo pastry tartlets, and some stuffed dates, I supplied a couple of bottles of wine and we toasted the beautiful Bayfield sunset.

Michael and I continue to meet secretly. We enjoy each other's company and there is nothing wrong with it although I wish that we could be more open.

I haven't seen Pierre for one month. It's funny, but I don't think that I really miss him anymore. Now that I have Rose and Michael the need for his company has diminished.

CHRISTMAS 2012

I went to the Salvation Army concert three weeks ago which really began the lead up to Christmas. Christmas in Bayfield was really early, November 8th but it was quite delightful with a long parade and marching bands. Oh, and the lights are so pretty. Rose and Tom insisted that I join them for Christmas. Their daughter, Jessica and family joined us. It was magical. I feel so happy.

MARCH 21ST. 2013

It is twenty-one years ago today that I lost my family, my name, and my whole identity. Today I heard that another person who gave evidence in the Criminal War Courts of The Hague and who was also in the Witness Protection Program, has gone missing. Pierre accidentally let it slip how concerned he was, and I then forced it out of him. Apparently, two men, both from Croatia, have disappeared. Pierre was visibly upset as he was their case worker. He refused to tell me more, but it is sufficient to say that it has got me scared. I thought that I would be safe in Canada.

MAY 18TH, 2013

Tom, Rose, and I joined the Croquet Club. We went to the Opening Season Cocktail Party at the Town Hall and met all sorts of interesting people. Everyone was so welcoming. I can hardly wait to learn how to play the game.

MAY 22ND, 2013

Rose and I had our first lesson at the Croquet Courts today. Tom, of course, appears to be a natural, probably because he plays golf, but Rose and I are equally hopeless. I cannot seem to get the right grip on the mallet.

I have offered to help Rose make canapés for her son's Canadian Wedding which is next week. We spent hours planning what to cook and I did so want to suggest some of my delicious Croatian dishes, but of course I could not. I feel bad not telling my dear friend my story, but I must never relax and tell the truth. It was my oath. I was sworn to secrecy when I joined the Witness Protection Plan.

JUNE 6TH, 2013

What a day! Rose and I worked like dogs all morning, but it was all worth it as the wedding buffet looked amazing. That little Japanese girl, Atsuko, is just like a painted doll. Oh my, what a beautiful wedding. I got to meet all three of Rose's children, Jessica, Anne, and Paul. A fantastic day.

Michael and I are still in love.

JUNE 20TH, 2013

Rose and I practiced croquet so much that we have decided to put our names down for the Tournament. I am beginning to get the hang of the game now. It is Golf Croquet today followed by a cocktail party at the Henderson's.

Pierre turned up unexpectedly late last night. He looked so weary. We talked about our relationship and I told him that I would like our affair to end. He owed it to his wife and children. As he left, he told me to be safe, which struck me as odd.

AUGUST 3RD, 2013

I have a strange feeling that I'm being watched. Once or twice, I've seen a black car drive up and down my street. The other day I swore that the same black car followed me to the Croquet Club. I keep thinking of Pierre's last words to me, 'Be safe.' Does he know something that I don't? I also can't help thinking about Pierre's other clients in the Witness Protection program some of whom have gone missing. I feel quite frightened, but I cannot tell anyone.

ROSE STARTED to close the journal when she noticed a business card tucked into the inside sleeve of the cover. She pulled it out and read the name. It was Pierre La Ville's home and business numbers.

Rose turned to Tom. "This Pierre La Ville knew there was someone out there killing off his clients so why didn't he tell the police? And how come he turned up here so soon after the murder? He told me that he was going to Ilderton and coincidently that was where the next victim was found. Tom, I have a bad feeling about Pierre la Ville".

Tom put the book that he was reading down and turned to Rose.

"Now, Rose, no more suspicious thoughts. Look, the police have one of the murderers in custody and the other one is dead. Why would Pierre be involved? Just leave it all to them, love, and don't get further involved."

Rose held the business card in her hand and then thoughtfully, with slow deliberation, she picked up the phone saying to Tom as she tapped in the number, "Well, at least I can talk to him and put my mind at rest."

The phone was picked up by a pleasant-sounding woman who introduced herself to Rose as Pierre's wife, Clare.

'I'm sorry. Pierre is away on business right now, but can I help you?"

"Oh, I just have some questions to ask your husband about a woman called Mary Stokes. Did you know her?"

There was a long pause before Clare spoke. "Who exactly did you say you were?"

"Oh, I'm so sorry, I didn't introduce myself but I'm Rose Blair. I live in Bayfield and Mary Stokes was my friend."

Clare replied quickly, "How strange. You said that you live in Bayfield? That is such a coincidence because I'm heading your way tomorrow for a 'Girls Getaway.' I belong to a friendship group made up of retired nurses, and we saw this weekend advertised and thought what a fun experience it would be to stay for a weekend together. I've never been to Bayfield, but it looks quite delightful on the web page. Look, I have quite a lot to tell you. Why don't we meet for coffee?"

Rose looked interested. She never expected that Pierre's wife would be so obliging.

"That would be great. Unfortunately, we don't have any places where we can go and just have coffee in the village which is a real shame. But why don't we meet for lunch at the Art See Café, say at 12:00 p.m. tomorrow?"

"Yes, that would be nice, but how will I know who you are?"

Rose thought for a minute and then said, "I'll wear a big, floppy yellow sun hat."

Tom rolled his eyes and gave Rose a lopsided smile.

"You never give up, my darling, do you?"

THIRTEEN

Susan looked around the bedroom suite where she had been staying at The Bayfield Village Inn. She had been so comfortable living there for two weeks. It was a shame to be packing up to leave although it would be good to get back to her little house in Wortley and, of course, to her two cats, Simba and Sara. She decided to go for one more final swim before heading out to the Lion's Hall and her last meeting with the team. She would miss the swimming pool dreadfully.

Fifty laps later Susan got out and towel dried her body. She glanced at her cell phone and noticed that she had missed one call from Rose Blair. She looked at her watch and realized that she would have to get her skates on otherwise she would be late for the final debriefing with her team. She would call Rose later.

The team seemed in high spirits which was always the way at the end of a successful investigation.

Susan grabbed a mug of coffee and sat down at the long conference table. She looked around the room at her team. Constable Mathieson with his youthful looks but keen eye for detail, Sergeant Flowers, conscientious and thorough leaving no stone unturned, and both Constables Elliot and Brown on secondment from the Goderich O.P.P. detachment.

She had enjoyed working with them and getting to know both men. She would surely miss the comradeship that working in a good team always fostered.

"Good morning, everyone. Today is our last day together and I want to congratulate you all on a job well done. The Serbian Syndicate is minus two of their most ruthless key players, Ljuba and Milo Strugar. Unfortunately, Milo still refuses to talk until his lawyer gets here from Montreal, but essentially the case has been signed, sealed, and delivered. Any questions?"

Sergeant Flowers stood up. He was a thorough and conscientious officer but tended to be a bit pedantic.

"Well, ma'am, can I get this straight. Ljuba and Milo were killing off witnesses who testified against their father, General Strugar, who was a Serbian General in the Croatian, Serbian, Bosnian war over twenty years ago. So, this was some kind of retribution? It all sounds a bit extreme considering their father was only given a seven-year prison sentence."

"Yes, Constable, it might appear extreme to us, but you have to understand the mentality of the Serbian Syndicate or any Mafia group. Vengeance is the key, that and 'saving face.' Don't try to equate our values with the likes of these gangsters."

Sergeant Flowers shuffled his papers around and then stood.

"Ma'am, what about the case worker, Pierre La Ville? If he knew that some of his clients from the Witness Protection were being murdered. Why did he not tell the police?"

"Good question, Sergeant. All I know is that when I talked to him, he said that all his client's names were strictly confidential, and he could not release any information about them. But you're right, it does seem strange that he didn't enlist our help. I will make a phone call to Inspector Le Bruin in Montreal and see if he can shed some light on the matter. Well, men, if you have no further questions, I need to write up my final report to the Chief. I'll copy you all in."

The team stayed around for a little longer. Constable Mathieson took down all the photographs of Mary Stokes which had been pinned to the wall and generally tidied up the Lion's Hall.

SUSAN WORKED AWAY on her laptop finalizing her report. She only remembered Rose Blair's phone call as she was putting her cell phone away in her purse and was preparing to leave. She tapped in Rose's number. Tom picked up the phone.

"Oh, hi, Tom, is Rose there?"

"Is this Susan? Well, Rose won't be back until after lunch. I'll get her to call you then."

Oh, well, Susan thought as she left The Lion's Hall, *I'll swing by this afternoon before I leave for London and bring them some wine and chocolates.*

IT WAS A NICE, warm, August day. A red Cardinal sat on one of the pear tree's branches and a large Blue Jay flew past as Rose wheeled her bicycle out of the garden shed. She had not done much cycling around the village recently, mainly because since Tom had bought his Audi it just seemed much quicker to pop into the village by car then to cycle everywhere. As she pedalled down Bayfield Terrace Rose felt free and happy, cycling had that effect on her.

She got to The Art See Café with ten minutes to spare. Sitting at one of the outside patio tables she adjusted her large, floppy, yellow sun hat. Looking around she saw an attractive forty something woman with short auburn hair approach the patio. She waved and the woman came over.

"Oh, hi. Are you Clare La Ville by any chance?" Rose got up and offered her hand.

"Hallo, yes, I'm Clare. What a gorgeous day."

The two women studied the menu and once the waitress had taken their orders they began to talk. Soon they both felt as if they had known each other for ages so much so that Rose was able to say, "Clare, do you know much about your husband's work?"

Clare answered frankly, "Rose, I know that all of his clients are strictly confidential, but I also know that Pierre has been having a series of affairs with some of his female clients for years."

Rose looked shocked. *So Mary Stokes was not his first indiscretion,* she thought.

"Don't look so shocked, Rose. You know he wasn't all that clever at hiding these affairs and a wife always knows when their husband is playing around."

Rose wondered if she would know if Tom was having an affair or not. She doubted that she would. She wouldn't even know where to begin, but she didn't want to get into that with Clare right now.

Clare continued, "The other strange thing about Pierre is that over the past ten years or so he has always seemed so flush with money. I thought, and still think, that he gets money from these women."

"Why have you remained married to him if you have known about his affairs for years?"

Clare's face clouded over, and a sadness veiled her beautiful eyes as she answered Rose frankly.

"Oh, Rose you sound so naive. We have stayed together because of the children, but just as soon as they are old enough to understand I'll be out of this marriage like a shot. There is no love between us anymore. He does his own thing and I do mine. Hence this fabulous girl's getaway. What a lovely village this is. You say that you actually live in this idyllic spot?"

Rose smiled. "Yes, Tom and I built our own house six years ago and, yes, we love living here. You must go to Pioneer Park this evening and watch the beautiful sunset. If you like walking there are three lovely trail walks, oh, and don't forget the shopping. There is a fabulous book shop, probably the best in Southern Ontario. It's called, "The Village Book Shop." You must go there too. What a shame that you are only here for such a short time. But back to Pierre, your husband. You say that he is on business? Does he leave you on your own much?"

Clare shrugged her shoulders. "Years ago, I would fly with him to Belgium when he went to meet with new clients. We would have a bit of a holiday together. Then when the children came along and school it wasn't quite so easy to get away. He goes to Europe once or twice a year but the rest of the time he's up and down the country visiting clients."

"You don't seriously think that he somehow gets money off his clients?"

Clare looked doubtful, "I don't know why I'm telling you all of this. I barely know you. Maybe I just want to get it all off my chest. In answer to your question, no, I seriously don't know where he gets the money. I just put two and two together and hoped that I'd get four, but you're right, most of his clients in the Witness Protection don't have two beans to rub together let alone any spare to give away."

"Have you actually ever asked him where he got the money?"

Clare's face darkened. "Yes, I once did, and he got angry and told me to mind my own business."

"Oh, well. There is probably some simple explanation."

Rose and Clare's lunch order arrived, and they stopped talking. Rose had ordered a Caesar salad and Clare, the quiche. The Art See Café always served excellent food.

The two women had hit it off really well. It was a shame that they didn't live closer. There still was, however, the question of Pierre and what he was up to. Intuitively Rose smelt a rat. She had omitted telling Clare about Mary's journal, and now she was more anxious than ever to speak to Susan.

"When does Pierre get back?" Rose asked as she glanced at her watch.

As she prepared to leave Clare answered, "Oh, he should be back in a couple of days. He's actually in your neck of the woods visiting one of his clients somewhere near Grand Bend. It was so nice chatting with you. Keep in touch." Clare squeezed Rose's hand as she left the café.

Rose waved goodbye, paid her bill, and, deep in thought, got on her bicycle to ride home.

SUSAN ARRIVED BACK at The Bayfield Village Inn just in time to check out and settle up her account. Before she left, she decided to give Henri Le Bruin a quick call. He picked up straight away.

'Henri, this is Susan. I have a problem and wondered if you could help?"

"Mais oui, ma cheri."

"English, Henri, speak English please."

"*Oui, cheri.* How can I help you?"

"Well, you know the case worker, Pierre La Ville, there seems to be some inconsistency here. He somehow appears to know more about the murders than he is saying. Can you run a complete background check on him, bank accounts, etc.? He is a loose string yet to be tied and I'm anxious to wrap up the case."

"*Certainment, ma cheri.* Oh, by the way, we had some communication from the customs men in Istanbul. It appears that our man Jim Reynolds is involved with a big smuggling cartel which they are hoping to break this evening. I will be in touch, *ma cheri,* just as soon as I have any information. *Au revoir.*"

Susan put her phone away and got in her car. Before leaving for London, she would swing by the LCBO and pick up a bottle of wine and then pop into Foodland and purchase some flowers or chocolates for Rose and Tom.

Rose and Susan arrived at Rose's house on Bayfield Terrace at almost the same time. Of course, Rose was on her bicycle and Susan in her plain, black police car but they greeted each other warmly.

"Oh, Susan, I'm so glad that you called by. I've got something for you to read and I do want to talk to you about Pierre La Ville."

Susan followed Rose into the house where they were effusively greeted by both Puff and Ben. Tom was nowhere to be seen.

"That's funny," Rose said, "Tom didn't say anything about going out and his car is still in the driveway. I wonder where he's got to?"

Susan followed Rose into the kitchen and then she remembered her conversation with Tom.

"I did talk to him at lunch time and he told me that you were out and would be back after lunch. Oh well, he's probably just gone for a walk. So, what did you phone me for, Rose?"

Rose had walked over to the desk where she had left Mary's journal. But she couldn't see it anywhere. She opened the desk drawers and then walked into their bedroom thinking that she may have left it by her bedside. But no. Susan followed her into the bedroom and asked, "Is anything wrong, Rose?"

"Yes, Susan, a journal belonging to Mary Stokes was sent to me. I wanted you to read it, but it seems to have disappeared."

"What was in it that you wanted me to see?"

"It appears that Mary and Pierre were having an affair although it had fizzled out before she met Michael Powell. I met with Pierre La Ville's wife, Clare today."

Susan interrupted Rose sharply, "What. You said that you met with Pierre's wife? How on earth did you arrange that?"

Rose smiled, "Oh that was simple. I found his business card tucked inside the journal. His wife's name is Clare and we met for lunch. Oh, I've got so much to tell you. Do you have a minute?"

After Rose had finished telling Susan all about her discussion with Clare, she threw her hands in the air and said, "Mary kept a detailed journal where she mentioned her relationship with Pierre and her suspicions about his knowledge of the murdered victims, all of whom were in the Witness Protection Program. It's so frustrating because I had the journal already to give to you and now it's gone."

The front door opened and to Rose's utter relief, Tom appeared. "Oh, there you are Rose, oh, and Susan. That's odd, I just dropped that journal off, the one that you asked for, Mary Stokes' journal."

Susan looked perplexed, "I never even knew about the journal let alone asked for it. Who actually did you speak to, Tom?"

Tom looked defensive, "This man phoned and said Inspector Parker would like to see the journal and could I please drop it off at the Lion's Hall. When I got there a pleasant enough man met me at the door, took the journal, thanked me, and that was that. How was I to know that you had not asked for it?"

Susan almost growled, "So, what did this man look like?"

"Oh, he was maybe in his late 40's or early fifties, tall, thin, dark hair, wearing a jacket, shirt and tie. Nice enough, well spoken, looked just like a cop."

Rose said, "That sounds like Pierre La Ville. I reckon that he's pulled a fast one on us, Susan. He must have guessed that I had Mary's journal. But one thing bothers me, Tom. Why did you not take your car?"

Tom smiled and said, "Well, you're always saying that I don't exercise enough so I thought that I would walk to the Lion's Hall. Nothing mysterious."

"Oh, Tom, you had me worried for a while. So, Susan, what do you think is going on? Pierre La Ville is obviously up to something. Where do you think that he's been getting this money from?"

"I don't know, Rose, but I mean to find out. Hopefully Inspector Le Bruin will be able to shed some light. Right, oh, I almost forgot, I brought you both this wine and some chocolates."

Susan left to drive back to London. She promised to contact Rose as soon as she had some information.

· · ·

ROSE PUT the kettle on for tea. She was very quiet. Tom came up behind her and wrapped her in his arms. "Penny for your thoughts, love?"

"Oh, Tom, I don't know what to think anymore. The police have the two killers, and I can understand the Serbian, Croatian vendetta although I can't condone it, but where does Pierre fit into all of this? His only connection is that he has been a case worker for his Witness Protection clients for years. Where did he get all that money from?"

Tom was pensive. "Rose, love, could he have been bought by the Serbian syndicate? How did the brothers know where to find the Croatians in the Witness Protection Program? Just maybe he supplied them with their addresses and in return received a generous payment?"

Rose jumped up and kissed Tom.

"Darling, you're brilliant. That's it, that's the deal I'm sure. It makes perfect sense. Oh, we must tell Susan."

"Hold on, my love, it's all just supposition. Look, Susan will work it out I'm sure and hopefully will be able to substantiate it with some solid proof. Now, let's just relax and put all of this behind us."

Rose kissed Tom once again and said, "Yes, you're right, my love. I've had my fill of intrigue and yes, I need to put it all to bed and get on with enjoying this glorious summer. Let's go into the sunroom and have a peaceful afternoon just reading. Come on Ben and Puff, time to relax."

Tom and Rose carried their tea into the sun lounge, their two dogs padded behind them with their tails wagging and as soon as Rose sat down on the sofa Ben jumped up and snuggled next to her and Puff curled up on the carpet at Tom's feet.

SUSAN HAD JUST ARRIVED BACK to her little house on Edward Street in Wortley Village when her phone rang. It was Henri.

"Susie, ma cheri. I have some information for you. Do you have some paper to write this down? I will email it to you later, too. According to Pierre's bank account several large sums of money have been paid in from that same registered numbered company used for the black Mercedes. In other words, the Serbian Syndicate. In total he has received $400,000 over a period of ten years. Has Milo Strugar made his statement yet? See if you can get him to implicate Pierre."

Susan let out a big breath. They had nailed him, well, almost. She replied to Henri slowly, "Milo's lawyer has just arrived from Montreal and he has cautioned Milo to say nothing. We're working on him now."

"Well, ma cheri, maybe if Milo knows that you are onto Pierre La Ville he might let slip more information. Bon chance, let me know when you've nailed him."

Susan put the phone down and went into the kitchen to feed her cats. They were getting very close to Pierre and then, hopefully, she could close the case for good.

FOURTEEN

The next day Susan had in her hands a full and concise statement from Milo Strugar. She read through it thoroughly and then picked up the phone.

"Henri Le Bruin."

He sounded so gruff, Susan thought but the minute he heard her voice he softened and gently said, "*Ma cheri, comment ca va?*"

"Henri, I thought that you would like to know that Milo Strugar finally gave a full statement. You were right. The minute that he was told we knew about Pierre La Ville's involvement, he opened up like a can of worms. I can now totally wrap up the case. Now, my darling, when can we celebrate?"

After her phone call to Henri, Susan decided to call Rose to give her the news. She tapped in her number.

"Oh, hi, Rose, Susan here. I've got some good news on the Mary Stokes murder. Do you want me to tell you?"

Rose laughed and said, "Well, first let me tell you what Tom and I think. We think that Pierre was being paid for information about his Croatian clients in the Witness Protection Program. Are we right?"

Susan gasped, "How did you guess? Yes, you're quite right,

he was paid handsomely for his information on the whereabouts of his Croatian clients. Lubja and Milo were professional hit men working for the Serbian Brotherhood, the old JNA. They were on a mission to avenge their father's betrayers who had taken the stand at the Criminal War Tribunal courts in The Hague. Men and woman were on the hit list and not all of them were part of the protection plan and not all were Pierre's clients. Between the two brothers they have been indicted for 18 counts of murder."

Rose interrupted Susan.

"So why was Michael Powell killed and why were Tom and I attacked?"

Susan continued. "Milo and Ljuba thought that you both knew Mary's Croatian past and as such you knew too much and would have to be eliminated. They were ruthless assassins - nothing would get in their way of revenge."

Rose continued to ask more questions.

"But who paid them? Who was the ultimate controller of these evil men?"

"The Serbian Brotherhood is like the Mafia, Rose. Money from old JNA supporters has been amassed in several different banks around the world. There is no one controller, the brotherhood works more like a cooperative and pay off money is always available. That is as much as we know but it is sufficient to put Milo away for many years."

Rose thanked Susan and put the phone down.

She called Tom over and told him the whole story. "So you see, Tom, you were right, clever you. Now let's go and have a cup of tea and relax in the sun lounge. I've got some reading to catch up on."

Tom and Rose had a lovely, peaceful afternoon just catching up on reading. Tom snoozed away while Rose curled up on the sofa devouring her latest book club book, 'The Book of Negroes', by Lawrence Hill. It was a brilliant read, and she could not put it down.

Their peace was shattered by the telephone ringing. It was Jessica. Rose answered, "Oh, hi, darling, how are you?"

There was a pause at the other end of the line and then Jessica let out a loud sob.

"Oh, Mom, Rob's left me, what shall I do..." and with that she began to sob even harder.

"Oh, my darling, my poor, poor darling," Rose murmured, her own heart breaking in two for her daughter's misery.

Jessica stopped sobbing and then blurted out:

"Mom, can the girls and I move in with you and dad in Bayfield...?"

Rose looked at Tom and then took a big breath before answering their daughter...

ROSE BLAIR'S RECIPES

Rose just loves to cook but she is not a very structured cook. Very rarely does she follow recipes accurately and is often known to substitute ingredients according to what she finds in her pantry or fridge. Rose believes in tasting as she goes along, adding and subtracting where necessary, particularly when it comes to seasoning. She has included many of the canapés that Mary and her prepared for Paul and Atsuko's wedding.

Fig and Goats Cheese tartlets

Ingredients
Phyllo pastry or small won ton squares
Goats cheese
Fig jam or fresh figs

Method
Using an upside-down muffin tray, small one, shape the phyllo pastry (or wonton wrappers) which have been cut into squares, brushed with melted butter and layered over the muffin cups. Bake in

hot oven, 375°F for about 10 minutes. Watch carefully as they will burn easily if left too long. Remove carefully when cooled. Place on serving plate and fill with 1 teaspoon of goat's cheese, top with fig jam or fresh figs cut in small pieces. Chill in fridge.

Stuffed Strawberries

Ingredients
Strawberries
Cream cheese
Icing sugar
Melted chocolate to drizzle

Method
Prepare strawberries by cutting off the pointy end. Cut the top off and gently scoop out enough flesh to form a little cup. Mix a small amount of icing sugar with the cream cheese, and stuff into hollowed out berry. Put the cut off top of the strawberry back on and drizzle melted chocolate over the top.

Bacon Wrapped Dates

Ingredients
Dates or water chestnuts or scallops
Bacon

Method
Wrap thin pieces of bacon around the dates. Put on parchment paper, bake in 350°F ovens for approximately 10 minutes until the bacon is crisp. You can do the same thing with water chestnuts. You

can also slit a date and fill it with cream cheese and serve chilled. Easy canapés to make.

English Scones
(Cranberry, orange, pineapple, ginger)

Ingredients
1 ½ cups flour
1/3 cup margarine or butter
2 tabs sugar
1 tsp. Baking powder
¼ cup milk or just enough to bind mixture to a pastry like texture.
Dried fruit of choice or mixture, grated orange peel if so desired.

Method
Mix to a pastry consistency (Rose puts all the ingredients into a food processor and zips it all up in a jiffy). Roll out or just pat down to a thickness of about 1'. Cut with a cookie cutter or shape in a circle and mark out sections with a knife - like spokes on a wheel. Brush with milk and bake in hot oven 375 for approx. 25 minutes or until golden.

Grandma's Spaghetti Pie
(Abby and Ella's favourite)

Ingredients
1 lb ground mince
1 chopped onion
beef stock
seasoning
2 cans spaghetti in tomato sauce

4 large potatoes

grated cheese

roux or white sauce= 1tab butter, 2 tabs flour, 2 cups milk, seasoning

Method

Fry onion, then mince, add stock, and cook until meat is cooked. Put in a large casserole dish. Open 2 cans of spaghetti, put on top of mince, layer cooked mash potatoes on top of that and finally pour white sauce on top, add grated cheese, and bake in oven 350°F for about 40 minutes.

Moussaka

Ingredients

1 eggplant sliced and pre roasted

1 lb ground mince

1 chopped onion

stock

6 sliced cooked potatoes

white sauce (see spaghetti pie)

grated cheese

Method

Cook ground mince like Spaghetti pie, layer mince, cooked egg plant, potatoes, mince etc. ending up with a layer of potatoes. Add white sauce and grated cheese and bake in 350°F oven for about 40 minutes.

Artisan Bread

Ingredients

3 cups warm water

6 cups flour

1 sachet of dried yeast or 2 dessert spoons yeast

1 dessertspoon salt

Method

Put salt in warm water, stir in yeast, add flour, stir until all flour is mixed well. Put the bowl with the dough in a plastic bag and leave in a warm place for 2 hours to rise. Take out a grapefruit size handful of dough shape to desired shape and leave for another hour. Put the remaining dough back in the plastic bag and refrigerate until more bread is required. Makes 3 loaves. Bake in hot oven of 400°F for about 30 minutes or until golden brown.

Lemon Meringue Pie

Ingredients

2 lemons

1 cup sugar

3 eggs yolks

1 tablespoon corn starch

1 cup water

Meringue Topping

3 egg whites

1 cup sugar

Pastry shell (Rose normally uses a bought one unless she has some pastry leftover from some other baking)

Method

Grate the zest of the 2 lemons

Squeeze juice from lemons, add 1 cup of water, stir in with sugar and flour until dissolved. Put saucepan over another pan of water (Bain Marie), slowly stir in 3 egg yolks, stir until thickened. Pour lemon mixture into pie case. Whisk egg whites until peaky (stiff) add sugar and whisk until stiff. Spread over lemon mixture. Bake in low oven heat, 300°F for 40 minutes.

Gazpacho (chilled tomato Spanish soup)

Ingredients
3lbs. (8 approx. ripe tomatoes)
1 green pepper
2 cloves garlic finely chopped
2 slices stale bread crusts removed
Olive oil, 1 tbsp.
4 tabs sherry vinegar (optional)
1-pint tomato juice
1 ¼ cups iced water
seasoning

For the garnish
1 small cucumber peeled and finely diced
1 small onion, finely chopped
1 red pepper seeded and finely diced.
2 hard boiled eggs
2 slices stale bread diced

Method
Skin tomatoes, quarter them, remove core and seeds, saving all the juices. Put the pepper in food processor, process for a few seconds. Add tomatoes, juice, garlic, bread, oil, and vinegar then process.

Season the soup then pour into a large bowl, cover and chill in fridge preferably over-night.

Prepare the garnishes. Heat the oil and fry the bread cubes until golden brown and crisp. Arrange in a small dish. Place remaining garnishes in small dishes. Before serving add iced water to the soup. The consistency should be thick but not too heavy. Serve with the garnishes.

Rich Chocolate (egg less) Walnut Cake
(Abby and Ella's favourite)

Ingredients
    3 cups flour
    2 cups sugar
    ½ cup cocoa
    2 teaspoon bicarb soda
    1 tsp. Salt
    2 tsp. Vinegar
    2 tsp. Vanilla
    1 cup oil
    2 cups warm water

Method
Mix together flour, sugar, soda, cocoa, and salt. Make 3 holes in the ingredients, pour vinegar in one hole, oil in second hole, and vanilla in the third hole. Pour water over all and mix well. Batter will be very thin. Pour into 2 greased cake pans, cook at 350°F for 30-40 minutes.

Fudge Icing

In microwave put in bowl 2 tabs. butter, melt. Add 1 tabs. cocoa, microwave 1 minute.

Stir in 1 cup icing sugar, stir in ¼ cup milk, and microwave 1 minute. Stir until thick and creamy. Pour in between cake and on top. Add walnut halves.

Jessica's Favourite Rhubarb Custard Pie

Ingredients
    2 ½ cups rhubarb
    2 tbsp. Flour
    2 egg yolks
    1 tbsp. Melted butter
    1 cup sugar
    1 pie pastry shell uncooked

Method
Beat egg yolks to a thick froth. Gradually add sugar, flour, and butter. Stir in rhubarb and pour into uncooked pastry shell. Bake in hot oven, 400°F for 15 minutes, reduce heat to 350°F and cook for another 30 minutes until the pastry is nice and brown.

Tom's Favourite Lemon Squares

Ingredients
    Base
    1 cup flour
    1/3 cup sugar
    1/3 cup margarine
    Topping

3 eggs
1 1/4 cups sugar
1 tbsp. Lemon rind
1/3 cup lemon juice
3 tbsp, flour
½ baking powder

Method

Pulse together in food processor the ingredients for the base. Combine until fine (or crumble with hands) Press into ungreased 8" square baking pan lined with foil or parchment paper. Bake for 12 minutes at 350 °F. Cool. In a bowl whisk together eggs and sugar until frothy, whisk in lemon juice and rind, stir in flour and baking powder. Pour mixture over cooked base. Bake for another 25-30 minutes. Let cool thoroughly. When cooled dust icing sugar on top and cut into small squares.

Leek and Potato Soup

Ingredients

1 leek
3 potatoes
stock (veg, beef or chicken)
1 onion
2 cups milk

Method

Cut onion and leek up. Peel and chop potatoes, put everything in saucepan, cover with water, and cook until tender. Add stock and milk, boil, and then simmer. Blend soup but leave some chunky bits of leak and potatoes. Serve hot with crusty bread or toast.

Steak and Guinness Pie

Ingredients
1 lb. steak
mushrooms
1 onion
beef stock or a stock cube
1 stick celery
1 bottle or can of Guinness
Puff pastry
½ cup flour

Method
Chop onion and mushroom, fry in a little oil, chop steak into inch cubes and toss in flour, and fry with onions and mushroom until brown. Add chopped celery and remaining flour, pour in Guinness (maybe have a small glass yourself) add stock cube, bring to the boil, then simmer for about 20 minutes. Put mixture in fairly deep pie dish. Roll out store bought puff pastry enough to cover the pie. Bake in a hot oven for about 30 minutes or until pastry is golden brown on top.

ACKNOWLEDGMENTS

Any errors and omissions of an historical or factual nature are mine and for this I humbly apologize.

I would like to thank my friends who read and edited, and my husband for his support and patience during the process of writing and editing this, my second full length novel.

A SNEAK PEEK AT MURDER AT THE TOWN HALL

Afterward, Rose could pinpoint the time when she knew, with certainty, that Tom was wavering in his love for her. She could see it in his eyes, his body language, and feel it in his touch. The biggest giveaway, however, was his reaction to Gillian Jeffries.

It was like an electric current had zapped through him when she walked in the room. His eyes lit up, his body straightened, and his whole demeanor softened taking years off his age. Rose hated Gillian Jeffries with a passion.

Tom and Rose had been having a quiet dinner at The Black Dog, a before the show repast. They had both ordered fish and chips and were just settling down to eat when Gillian walked in.

Taller and slimmer than Rose, Gillian wore her glossy chestnut coloured hair cascading down her back like a horse's mane. She wore a tight fitting low necked sweater and equally slinky fitted black pants. There was a feline quality to her that instantly warned the females of the species to be on red alert.

Gillian had moved to Bayfield just over a year ago after a messy divorce from Andy Jeffries, an accountant from London. She had opened a fitness centre in the village called Time for Toning and it seemed that half of the men of Bayfield had taken out a membership, including Tom.

At first Rose had been amused at Tom's enthusiasm for fitness. After all, the only exercise that he had practised was in the summer when he played endless games of golf and sailed his boat. Rose had even encouraged and praised his dedication towards working out at the new gym. Every morning at 7:45 a.m., Tom would religiously jog over to the fitness centre. Gillian, the instructor, had told all her clients that if they lived within a 3km distance of Time for Toning she expected them to jog or at least walk as part of their fitness regime. Just like a puppy dog, Tom had obeyed his mistress, much to Rose's amusement.

It wasn't until three months into the program that Rose started to feel a little uncomfortable about Tom's dedication to fitness. She did, however, find out that some of her friends whose husbands had also enrolled into Time for Toning were beginning to feel irritated. Maybe they were all equally in Gillian's thrall and if that was the case, like all infatuations, it would fade, and no harm would be done.

It was February and the village was gripped in the middle of one of the fiercest winters that anyone had witnessed, at least in the past fifty years. Feet of snow covered the ground, and the trees were coated in what looked like pristine white cake icing dripping down in fingers of snow. Highway 21 had been closed several times already with freezing rain and white out conditions fit for the arctic.

There had been some concern over whether the band that had been booked to play at the Town Hall would even make the drive from Toronto to Bayfield as the previous day had seen a dreadful blizzard and temperatures had plummeted to an all-time low of minus thirty-two. Rose, a new member of the Town Hall committee, had offered to put any of the band members up should they not want to drive back after the concert. She hadn't heard if her offer had been taken, but she had prepared the guest room just in case it was needed.

Tom and she were looking forward to the concert, as The Berries had been one of their favourite groups way back in the 70s. Joe Berry, the lead singer had been quite the dish in his day. Most of Rose's friends had a crush on him and if it hadn't been that Rose was madly in love with Tom at that time, she too would have joined the ranks of the smitten.

It was with a sigh of relief when word got out that the band had finally arrived in Bayfield and were currently eating dinner at The Albion. Rose looked at her watch and turned to Tom who was just finishing off his fish and chips.

"Tom, it's already seven o'clock. We should get going. The glasses have to be put out and I would like to be there to meet and greet the band. What was the name of the supporting group?"

Tom looked thoughtful. "Well love, you should know as you're on the committee, but I do remember you telling me that they had booked a harpist called Cynthia for the supporting act. Do you know if she has arrived yet?"

"I don't know. I'll just phone Peggy as I'm sure that she'll know."

Rose pulled out her Samsung. Tom had given it to her the previous summer, and it had literally saved her life when she had been attacked on the beach. She now held the phone in great reverence and always promised Tom that she would leave it powered up and ready for emergencies.

Peggy answered the phone crisply. As Rose asked her question, she could just picture the chairwoman with her clip board crossing off the 'to-do' list. Peggy was a super-efficient and lovely woman and Rose held her in great esteem.

"Well Rose, no need to worry. I have Cynthia here at the Town Hall tuning up her harp as I speak. Everything's under control, although we are waiting for Tom to set out the bar and bring up the wine glasses."

Rose put her phone away and hurried Tom into finishing off his Guinness. As they left The Black Dog, she looked over her shoulder and caught Gillian Jeffries eye. She smiled sweetly at Rose and wiggled her fingers at Tom.

Tom had put his 'man-toy' sports car into storage for the winter. Rose had suggested that they walk to the pub from their house on Bayfield Terrace. As they left The Black Dog the chilling cold air numbed their faces. They trudged through the thick, dirty snow piled up on each side of the road. Rose held onto Tom's arm tightly. She did not want to fall and break her leg like her friend Wendy had four weeks ago. It had totally incapacitated her and made her house bound and reliant on her husband and friends.

They safely arrived at the Town Hall which looked particularly beautiful with its snow topped roof and twinkling outside lights. Rose immediately went upstairs to help with the collecting of tickets and Tom disappeared downstairs to retrieve the glasses.

It was seven-fifteen, and The Berries were due to perform at about eight-thirty with Cynthia, the harpist, scheduled to play as an opener at eight p.m.

People started to trickle in soon after Rose and Tom had arrived. There was still no sign of the band as yet, but Cynthia had come back down to the basement and was introduced to Rose by Peggy.

"Rose, meet Cynthia McArdle. She's from Halifax, Nova Scotia. Isn't that where your daughter Anne lives?"

At the mention of Anne, Rose's heart quickened. They were all on tenterhooks as the baby was due in the next week or two, the first week of March was the date that Anne had given her to keep free.

Anne, and her partner Alan, a Professor of Astrophysics at Dalhousie, seemed blissfully happy. The pregnancy had gone smoothly and now it was just a waiting game. Rose had of course promised to fly out to Halifax and help with the baby as soon as it was born. They had last seen their daughter the previous summer when she had first introduced them to Alan and then had proceeded to announce that they were expecting a baby.

That had all happened at the same time as when her good friend, Mary Stokes, had been murdered at the Croquet Club and their lives had been turned upside down with the subsequent events. Even thinking about the murder all these months later made Rose shiver. How could she ever forget finding her friend's body slumped over the grave with a crossbow bolt pierced through her body?

Thankfully they had had a quietish winter to recover, although there had also been the upheaval of Jessica, their oldest daughter, who had dropped the bombshell that her marriage to Rob was on the rocks. Fortunately, that had proved to be a storm in a teacup and after only a three-day separation, Rob had rushed in and declared his undying love to Jessica and had whisked their daughter and grand-children away.

Now Rose and Tom were preparing to look after Abby and Ella over the March Break while Rob and Jessica had a second honeymoon in Cuba. *Let's just hope that Anne has had her baby before then and not while Abby and Ella are staying with us,* Rose thought as she looked more closely at Cynthia McArdle.

At first glance she appeared to be a young thing in her twenties, but then, on closer inspection Rose realized that she was looking at a very good face lift. The tell-tale tucks at the side of her face were the giveaway, plus her neck, which she garnished with a colourful scarf. Rose glanced at Cynthia's hands, another age giveaway. She now reassessed her age at somewhere over fifty. She realized with a jolt that Cynthia had been speaking to her. She shook her head and smiled saying,

"I'm so sorry. I was miles away in Halifax thinking about our daughter. Forgive me for not listening. Oh, by the way, did Peggy offer you accommodation with us tonight? I've made up the guest room. If you don't mind being around dogs, we would love to have you spend the night."

Cynthia beamed a fantastic smile showing small, pearly white teeth. She was a strange looking woman, not conventionally attractive but certainly quite enigmatic in her own way.

"I would love to take you up on your kind offer. It would only be for tonight as I was planning, weather permitting of course, to go and visit my aunt in Clinton. I promised her that I wouldn't leave this area without a visit. My plane back to Halifax doesn't actually leave until Tuesday."

They were interrupted by the band arriving. By now it was almost seven-thirty. *They are cutting it a bit fine*, Rose thought as she watched the four-man band walk in carrying their guitars and gear, stamping snow off their shoes, and laughing amongst themselves. From snippets of conversation, they had obviously had a few beers at The Albion before coming to the Town Hall.

The four men, two of them in their fifties or even early sixties, wore casual blue jeans and black sweatshirts. Three of the men had shoulder length hair and looked distinctly like aging hippies. The youngest of the band reminded Rose of their son, Paul. He looked about the same age and had a pleasant freshness about him. Rose instantly recognised Joe Berry, the lead singer.

He looked more like George Clooney now with his salt and pepper hair and rugged face. He was still a heart stopper. If their daughter Anne was around, she would say that Joe was 'fit', but maybe not, as he was probably too old for her generation.

Peggy welcomed them effusively and asked Rose if she could show the band downstairs where they had set out sandwiches and beer for them.

"Follow me", Rose said, and the four men traipsed downstairs with Rose in the lead.

"The washrooms are here," she said pointing to the side of the hallway. "Men's are to the left and women's to the right. Of course, you don't really need to know that. You can use any of them," she added to a chuckle from Joe.

They continued to walk through the hallway towards the back where the meeting room was located.

"The kitchen is here. There are glasses on the shelves if you want some water although we have laid out refreshments on the table for you."

When they entered the meeting room, Cynthia McArdle jumped up and made a bee line to greet Joe Berry.

"It's been a long time, Joe," she said. Rose interrupted them before she could say anything else.

"Right, well, if you need anything, I'll be upstairs. See you all later." With that she went to leave. It was already very late. She should have been taking tickets at the door by now.

Rose saw Tom putting glasses out on a tray in the kitchen as she was returning upstairs. She waved to him and almost bumped into Gillian Jeffries making her way downstairs.

"We meet again, Gillian. Can I help you? Are you looking for anything?"

Gillian's face was flushed, and her eyes looked wild. She nodded quickly and said that she was looking for the washroom. Rose pointed the way and continued on her way upstairs to take up her position collecting tickets.

The hall soon started to fill up. There were a number of people that Rose knew mostly from the Croquet Club. She spotted Lena, from the Historical Society, and Angela, the librarian. She looked around to see if she could find Gillian Jeffries but there appeared to be no sign of her yet. Cynthia was about to go on the stage to start her performance. Rose wondered why Gillian was taking so long to return. Was she with Tom?

Tom had just finished loading up his second tray of glasses when he was halted in his tracks by the sound of voices. There were two people arguing out in the hallway besides the kitchen. He recognized right away the voice of Gilly, but the other, a man's voice, he could not place.

He couldn't hear what they were saying, but it certainly did not sound like a friendly discussion. Then it went very quiet, and Tom felt that he could leave the kitchen undetected and carry the glasses upstairs.

As he walked into the hall, he bumped into one of the band members coming out of the men's washroom. Tom smiled at him and continued on his way upstairs. He glanced at his watch as he put the tray of glasses onto the bar table. It was eight-ten and Cynthia the harpist was in full swing. The gentle, rippling music gripped the audience and Tom could see that Cynthia was certainly very professional.

Rose sidled up to Tom and asked if he had seen Gillian Jeffries. He whispered that yes, she had been downstairs arguing with some-one, but he didn't know where she had got to after that incident. Rose looked at her watch. It was almost 8:30 p.m. The Berries would soon be on stage.

Cynthia played on and the audience quietened as they were captured by the gentle rhythmic plucking of the harp's strings. She played beautifully and with such feeling. Rose was lulled by the last melody. It seemed to be a combination of *Greensleeves* intermingled with a Celtic beat, an unusual mix but very haunting. Rose was prodded out of her reveries by Peggy who looked agitated. Immedi-ately Rose could see that something was wrong.

"Rose, please come out into the lobby. I need to talk to you," she whispered.

Rose quickly exited the auditorium and met Peggy in the lobby by the front door.

"What's up, Peggy?"

She looked a nervous wreck.

"Joe Berry has gone missing and they're meant to be performing in a few minutes."

Rose thought quickly.

"Well, when Cynthia's finished, we can have a short intermission and hopefully Joe will turn up by then. Has anyone seen him?"

Peggy answered quickly. "Yes, I spoke to him when he first arrived and then you took the whole band downstairs and that was the last time that I saw him."

"He seemed in good spirits and the rest of the group all appeared quite relaxed." Rose said while she tried to remember what was actually said when she had showed them around.

"Peggy, I presume that you've looked outside? He might have gone out for a cigarette?"

Peggy answered that they had indeed looked outside, and no, he wasn't anywhere to be found. Bill Branson, the lead guitarist, was the only band member that smoked, and he had stepped outside for a cigarette at around eight o'clock.

Cynthia concluded her last piece of music and the curtains closed to tremendous applause. Peggy dashed back into the auditorium and announced that there would be a fifteen-minute intermission. Hopefully, that would be time enough to locate Joe Berry.

Peggy and Rose both went downstairs while Tom continued to pour out the wine and take orders from the audience. Both Rose and Tom had taken the online Smart Serve course and were, therefore, allowed to work on the cash bar. The Town Hall committee had applied for the liquor license one month before. Susan and Jeff, both long time committee members who held their Smart Serve accreditation, had gone away as snowbirds for the winter leaving no one on the committee legitimately allowed to man the bar. That was when Rose had volunteered Tom and herself to take the online course and now they were in great demand.

It was Peggy who found him. He had been pushed into the tiny jail in the Town Hall basement. A kitchen knife protruded from his neck. Blood had splattered everywhere. It was the iron-tinged smell of the copious amounts of blood that had first drawn Peggy to peer into the old jail in the basement.

Rose was closest to her when she let out a piercing scream, a noise so curdled that Rose fairly shook with fear herself. She had run over from the washrooms and found Peggy ashen faced and quivering in shock as she pointed her shaking finger towards the jail room. Rose had run over but had been halted in her steps by the sight before her. It was Joe's eyes that she would see repeatedly in her dreams over the next few weeks.

They seemed to be fixed on her in an accusing way. His mouth was clamped shut and his one hand gripped the knife handle as if he was trying to pull the deadly weapon out. He was clearly dead. Rose recognized the knife as one that the Town Hall had bought in a bid to revamp the kitchen. Indeed, it looked very much like one of the set that Rose herself had purchased only two weeks ago from Kulpeppers in Goderich.

"Oh my gosh, Peggy, oh my gosh. Ummm... I'll call the police." Rose stammered. She might as well have been talking to herself, as Peggy just stood there in a trance like state. Rose pulled out her phone and tapped in the numbers, 911. A computer voice answered, "Which service are you calling?"

Rose half whispered, "A man is dead. We'll need an ambulance and the police. Please come quickly."

After providing the location and her name she put her phone away and went over to Peggy. She wrapped her arms around her and gently guided her into the meeting room where the three remaining band members were sitting. In a dead pan voice Peggy quietly said, "I'm afraid we have some bad news. I found Joe, but it appears that he has been murdered. I have to go upstairs to make an announcement to the audience, but the police have been called and I am sure that they will want you all to stay here."

Peggy shook her head as if shaking away the horror of the scene she had just witnessed. She turned to leave and then suddenly slumped as if all her energy had evaporated. She spoke softly to Rose with a quivering voice. "Would you mind Rose, telling everyone what's happened. I really don't feel up to it. I feel quite faint. Thank you my dear."

Rose fetched a glass of water from the kitchen and turned to leave The Berries and Peggy sitting in shocked silence. She raced upstairs, being careful not to look at the jail, and found Tom working feverishly taking people's orders.

Doug had volunteered to help, and the two men poured out wine and handed out beers like professional bar men. Rose walked up to the stage picked up the microphone which had been set up for Cynthia the harpist.

"Ummm... good evening everyone. I have an unpleasant announcement to make. The Berries will not be able to perform tonight due to tragic circumstances."

Rose felt her voice thicken and tears spring to her eyes, but she soldiered on. "The lead singer has been found dead and the police are on their way. Please, nobody can leave the hall as I'm sure that that the police will want to question everybody."

Rose took a moment to look around the auditorium. She could see Gillian Jeffries looking in an obvious state of shock. She must have come into the auditorium while Rose was helping Peggy look for Joe Berry because she was certain she was not there before. There was a general murmur of shocked whispers as people settled back in their chairs waiting for the police to arrive. Tom beckoned to Rose who walked over to him in a daze. He put his arms around her and pulled her close to him.

"Are you alright, my love? You look dreadful. Was it you who found Joe?"

"No, Peggy found him and she's in an awful state. Oh Tom, it was horrendous. I cannot get rid of the image of him all covered in blood with a knife protruding from his neck. His dead eyes just stared accusingly at me." Rose felt her voice quiver as big, glistening tears started to roll down her cheeks. *I must try to hold it together*, she thought as she fished in her pocket for a tissue. Taking a big gulp of air, Rose wiped her eyes and asked Tom for a glass of wine.

When Susan received the call from the Goderich O.P.P. detachment she couldn't believe it. Another murder in Bayfield! It had been less than six months since she had investigated the murders of Mary Stokes and Michael Powell. How could such a small village harbour so much evil? With that thought in mind Susan had grabbed her bag and jumped into her car prepared to drive the eighty-minute journey from her house in Wortley Village, London, up to Bayfield.

The air was crisp and fresh snow had fallen covering the roads like fine talcum powder. *At least it wasn't a blizzard*, thought Susan who was used to driving in all weather conditions. Hopefully she would arrive at the Town Hall before ten o'clock.

Just over an hour later as she pulled into Clan Gregor Square, Susan was amazed at the activity in front of the Town Hall. An ambulance stood immediately in front with its lights flashing, which Susan found ironic as this was after all, a dead body, not an emergency.

Yellow police tape, fluttering in the wind, marked off the whole front of the Town Hall and police officers kitted out in disposable white coveralls with hoods and masks, were already going about their business. Susan searched for somewhere to park. She finally plumbed for parking in front of Brandon's Hardware Store and walked over to the Town Hall. She was about to pass under the yellow tape when an officer came over and blocked her entry. Susan recoiled. She had never been stopped from entering a crime scene before.

She fished in her bag for her warrant card and held it up to the

Constable. "I'm Inspector Parker from Serious Crimes and I have driven all the way from London to be here tonight. I could have left it until tomorrow, but in murder cases it is imperative to see the scene of the crime first-hand before it gets tampered. I sincerely hope that your team of men have not tampered with the evidence. Now please, let me through. I have work to do."

The officer stood back and ushered her through.

As Susan entered the building, the crime scene photographer was just leaving. They almost bumped into each other. Susan grabbed his arm.

"Excuse me; I don't think that we've met before. My name is Detective Inspector Susan Parker, I will be leading this investigation and so I would appreciate it if you could make sure I get copies of the photographs forwarded to me. I expect we will be setting up an Incident Room in the village"

The man looked somewhat taken aback, but he politely held out his hand and said, "My name is Peter Joyce. I was asked by the Goderich O.P.P. Detachment to come out to record the scene of the crime. I always like to use a traditional SLR with roll film as well as a digital camera. I'm of the old school; digital can get deleted or played around with whereas traditional film photography never tells lies."

He smiled and suddenly his face changed from just ordinary to amazingly handsome. Susan's heart missed a beat.

"Oh, well, if you can get the photographs to me as soon as possible that would be great. Here's my card with my contact particulars and a secure email address. Now I must go and see with my own eyes what horrors await."

Peter Joyce loaded his old Olympus SLR and his modern digital video recorder into his battered, old Jeep. He watched as Susan nodded to the attending officer who took her name and let her through into the hall. DI Susan Parker had intrigued him. He would ask around and find out more about the attractive woman who commanded such a senior position in the police force.

As she entered the hall, Susan had glanced over towards the fire hall and the neighbouring Lion's building which, in the past, she had been able to use as an incident room.

It was a convenient location, and she crossed her fingers that if needed it would once again be available for her use.

The poster in the glass display box by the front door of the Town Hall showed four men, older men at that, with the name The Berries. A 'Sold-Out' sticker had been stapled over the poster. She walked into the Town Hall and was immediately hit by a stream of heat. Susan undid her thick overcoat and walked up the steps to where her old friend Rose Blair stood talking to her husband, Tom. There was something about Tom that Susan found immensely attractive and she wasn't quite sure what it was.

He wasn't conventionally handsome, and he wasn't overtly manly, but the chemistry between them ignited whenever she was near him and somehow, she could not quell it. Rose turned from Tom and seeing Susan, rushed over to greet her, making Susan instantly feel guilty about her thoughts for Tom.

She had been best friends with Rose all through their university days spent at Queens in Kingston. After graduation they had both gone their separate ways, Rose to Tom and a happy marriage, Susan to a disastrous relationship followed by a divorce and a major change of career.

She had crawled up the ladder, a predominantly male one at that, and had reached the position of Detective Inspector by sheer hard work and tenacity alone and was now getting close to retirement. Susan smiled warmly at her friend Rose.

"Susan, I wish that we didn't always have to meet under such dreadful circumstances. How are you?"

Out of the corner of her eye, Rose noticed a flash of light sparkle from Susan's finger. "Oh my gosh, Susan! You're wearing an engagement ring!"

Susan blushed as she waved her hand in front of her friend. "Henri and I got engaged at Christmas. But right now, dear Rose, I must get to work. I'll tell you all about it later. Now, show me the body."

The two women went downstairs to the jail. The investigation into Joe Berry's death had begun.

ABOUT THE AUTHOR

Over the past thirty years Judy has written twenty novellas, various collections of poetry and a number of plays. Judy wrote her first full length novel in 2013 and developed it into a series called the Rose Blair Murder Mysteries all set in the sleepy village of Bayfield on the beautiful shores of Lake Huron in Ontario, Canada.

Judy and her husband reside in Bayfield with their beloved dog Susie and cat Thomas and enjoy visits from their children and grandchildren.

After retiring Judy and her husband took on a new challenge in their lives. Purchasing land on the outskirts of Bayfield they have planted a six acre vineyard.

Life is beautiful and sweet. I feel so very blessed with all my wonderful family and friends who continually surround me with their love.

www.ingramcontent.com/pod-product-compliance
Lightning Source LLC
Chambersburg PA
CBHW051510170626
46811CB00002B/731